WEAKNESS

IS

PROVOCATIVE

BOOK FOUR OF THE CLOVIS ACADEMY LEGACY

Ross Harringway

Omega Press
El Paso, Texas

CLOVIS ACADEMY LEGACY: BOOK FOUR

WEAKNESS IS PROVOCATIVE

OMEGA PRESS

An imprint of Omega Communications Group, Inc.

For information contact:

Omega Press
5823 N. Mesa, #839
El Paso, Texas 79912

FIRST EDITION

Printed in the United States of America

OTHER BOOK BY THE SAME AUTHOR

Clovis Academy Series

Reign of Death

Forbidden Region

Shadows in the Dark

PROLOGUE

The death of Cush Rosenburg had been an event that left a lasting impression on all of his siblings and nieces and nephews. Cush was a medical doctor with advanced experience in duplication of life forms through cloning. He was equally talented in the in vitro process to create children. He spent practically his entire medical career serving his father, Alfred, at the Rosenburg Ranch on planet New Edinburgh. Cush impregnated hundreds of women; most of them had not been willing participants, with his father's sperm. He also had created thousands of cloning tubes, using stolen alien blueprints and technology, so that perfect duplicates of his family members could be stored away in safe keeping for future use.

But Cush made one fatal error. He had decided that he wanted to make children of his own. In that endeavor,

Cush began to inseminate half of the women brought to him with his own sperm and the other half with his father's sperm. Cush was able to get away with his deception for a few years. But on one fateful day, his father discovered that Cush had been committing what was referred to as "an unforgivable act."

Alfred went into an uncontrollable rage, almost like a three year old throwing a temper tantrum, and had his assassins, the Ragnarsson's, arrest Cush and bring him to the family mansion for execution. The patriarch of the Rosenburg family forced all of his children to watch as Cush was sliced apart and tortured to the end of his endurance. Cush begged for his life and for mercy. After an hour of the brutality that he had suffered, Cush begged for death. Alfred eventually granted that request and had Cush disemboweled in front of his siblings.

Alfred instructed his son Matthew, another medical doctor, to take over the in vitro clinics and then appointed his daughter Nicolette to run the cloning operation. Nicolette had finished her medical degree the year before Cush was murdered and she had worked under his tutelage in the belly of an abandoned alien space craft that was under the purple sands of New Edinburgh. She learned everything that she needed to know regarding the cloning process from Cush and was fully capable of replacing him as the chief of that area.

But Nicolette had carried a grudge against her father ever since the day he killed Cush. There had been a very close bond between the siblings, one that Nicolette kept from her father and his constantly scheming wife, Magdalena. Nicolette kept an even bigger secret from her father and that was the fact that she had secured a few vials of blood from Cush's corpse. She used his DNA and created a few hundred clones of Cush and hid them in her personal Raumschiff that was secured at her personal mansion. No one could access her space craft without the proper codes, so Nicolette was certain that her actions would go undetected.

But she had been wrong. One of her family members had been astute enough to figure out her game and confronted her one morning while they were alone. They were walking down one of the light pink concrete paths through one of the parks that had been built by Alfred Rosenburg. They were surrounded by tall trees with orange and yellow leaves and many gardens, separated from the trees and the path by a two foot high red, white and pink brick wall that protected endless rows of multi-colored flowers. It was a peaceful area where a person could find solace or two people might share secrets without the fear of being recorded.

"I know what you did Nikki," Penelope Rosenburg had accused her as they walked side by side, kicking the fine granulated purple sands as they walked.

"What are you talking about, Penny?" Nicolette acted as if she had nothing to hide, but was nervous since Penelope was the smartest of all her siblings.

"You are making clones of us without father's approval," Penelope whispered. "Don't worry, I will not tell father. I hate him for what he did to Cush. I hate him for what he forced me to go through to change my appearance. I want to help you."

Nicolette stopped in her tracks and looked at her sister with a piercing gaze. They were both silent for a few moments before Nicolette began to speak again.

"All right, Penny. How can you help me?"

"I have a massive amount of unused space in the bottom storage rooms at the Baroness Hotel. We could store the clones you are making there, where Magdalena and father will never see them."

"If we get caught, they will kill you."

"They will kill us both, Nikki. I really do not care if I die, but I think we should have replacement clones ready to replace father and Magdalena one day. I am worried about their actions. They exert no authority over our siblings that have openly demonstrated a propensity for violence. Caine, Peter, Thomas and David are dangerous men. Nydia is not emotionally well and continues to sleep with rogues and criminals. Caine and Peter are the most concerning with their sadistic acts. One day they will cause too much attention to be brought down on all of us. I have voiced my concerns to father and he has told me to mind my own business. He does not care that their actions could bring attention to our entire family."

Nicolette nodded in agreement with her, "Rebecca and Nydia are just as out of control as they are. I am glad that at least two of us care. Kristen cares as well and she is with me. The three of us can begin to slowly accumulate an army of clones at the Baroness and make our plans. Penny, this must stay between the three of us. I do not trust any of our other siblings."

"Even Matthew?"

Penelope was surprised given that at one time in their childhood, Matthew and Nicolette had been inseparable.

"Especially him. Matthew is terrified of being killed by father just as Cush was. Matthew has no loyalty to the family, but he is loyal to himself and his own self-preservation. He would sell us out to father to save his own ass. Tell no one."

"All right, Nikki. Just us three girls."

"Penny, you need to know that the cloning process is a twofold action. The physical body can be created in those alien machines. But it does not duplicate the mind. The memories and everything that we are in our heads is lost. The Replicant bodies are mindless and need to have their brains filled with the memories and knowledge by way of computer transfer. Since I was not able to download Cush's brain prints, all of his clones are bodies waiting for a mind."

"So we need to find some willing people to let us do what?"

"No, not living people, Penny. We need to find people that are dying or dead and scan their memories, steal them and then transplant their entire knowledge and memories into the brains in the clones of Cush."

"I have never seen any dead people on the space station so that might be difficult."

"People die up there all the time, Penny. We just have to be in the right place at the right time. We need to use the minds of people that are good citizens, Penny. We need to be very selective and screen the dying persons before we use them. We do not want to give a psychopath a second chance at life. But a good woman or a good man? Yes, absolutely. We need to find those people."

Penelope crossed her arms and looked up into the sky. "You are correct about the deaths. The bar fights on Cy-7 usually result in casualties. But most of them are not people we would want to use. We need special men and women that had goals, drive, determination and aspirations to be decent. Those are the people we need to find."

"I will teach you everything you need to know, Penny. Sometimes opportunity strikes when you least expect it and we must be ready. Good people die every day. When you come across one or more of such people do not hesitate to act."

Penelope smiled at her sister, "Nikki, I will do everything that you tell me to do."

"Then let's walk back to my mansion so I can teach you the science behind DNA collection and brain pattern duplication. You need to see the machinery for yourself so that you can gauge how much space is needed to store it all and to have a replication laboratory that will comfortably fit us and the clones at the same time."

"Who else knows how to work the machinery to

create the duplicates?"

Nicolette stopped walking as a group of slave Kotek children ran past them on their way to their preparatory school. She waited until they were far past them so that they could not overhear the conversation with their enhanced hearing abilities.

"Just me, Matthew, Kristen, David, father, Uncle John and the Professor. There is some other medical staff that have seen the machinery and even assisted in the creation of clones, but none of them have been taught how to make a perfect human duplicate like I can. Cush was rightfully selective in who he confided in."

"So, if we do this together, are there any others we can trust?"

Nicolette nodded her head in the affirmative, "There are very few people that would be willing to stand with us, but there are some. Juliana and Kristen are two of our sisters that might break ranks and help us. But under no circumstances should we trust anyone from Uncle John's side of the family. They are always so secretive and elusive. They scare me, Penny."

Penelope sat down on the brick wall and looked over the beautiful array of flowers behind her. "They should scare you, Nikki. I have been to Sikorsky's Planet and Semiramis. I have seen the things that John has been involved in designing. They have weapons that are more powerful than ever created before. The scariest part of their projects is that John and the Professor would not hesitate in using them on people. They have no empathy for others. Eventually, you and I will have to face them. What I saw on Semiramis was very disturbing. They have dozens of factories creating new fleets for the Glorious Leader. Mind you I am not talking about fleets of the Battle Cruisers as we know them. These ships are ten times the size of the average Battle Cruiser. Most of the factories on Semiramis are underground to avoid detection from errant space ships. But some of the above ground facilities were spotted a few times which prompted Uncle John to have the ships shot down and the passengers executed."

"That is why they call the orbiting moon over Semiramis the Blood Moon? Uncle John has been the cause of those tragedies?"

"Yes," Penelope nodded. "John thinks that humanity must be ready for some war against some alien race. He never elaborated to me what he meant. But the salient point is that if and when John gets those ships operational, they would be able to crush any and all rebellions. Normal Battle Cruisers would be like ants to these other ships."

Nicolette sat down next to her and touched a full bloomed pink flower that was in the vast garden surrounding them. "To think we as a species can build a garden like this with so much beauty and serenity and yet, at the same time, we willingly build weapons of such destructive power. I cannot see how we reconcile that dichotomy."

"We don't reconcile it, Nikki. We fight the evil ones to the death. Remember the motto of the Glorious Leader is that weakness is provocative. As long as good women like us stand by and do nothing, those with bad intent will not cease their actions. They will be emboldened by our lack of resistance. There comes a time in life when the good people must rise up and fight. I have a feeling this may be that time."

"Against all of our family, Penny? We are descendants of the Glorious Leader. How do we fight our own blood?"

Penelope sighed and stood up, "Most of our extended family only care about position and power. How do we fight them? I am not sure, Nikki. I am a financial analyst, not a military tactician. We need to find women and men that do know how to fight and get them to join us."

"Easier said than done."

"Perhaps in time we will meet such individuals and we can join with them," Penelope said hopefully. "Perhaps one day we can help to end all of the suffering of the people."

"Most of the people would not even care whether they had freedom or not, Penny. They are too stupid to know that they are being oppressed."

"Well, neither one of us can ever fix stupid. But we can at least get those that have some ability to reason to recognize that the oppression of our family is not the best form of government out there. There is a better way. There has to be a better way. Together we can search for a better direction for everyone."

"I'm in."

CHAPTER ONE

The sand storm had passed over Clovis City by the early morning. There was much evidence of the destructive force of the winds left behind in the city. One building that was half-way completed had been blown down. The metal frames, brick, synthetic materials and concrete had been ripped out of the ground and flung in every direction. One metal brace, about three hundred feet high and five feet wide had smashed into a housing area. Two families were killed by the large metal brace, the lucky ones died on impact. The rest were swept up into the powerful winds, thrown into the air, dying as their bodies were crashed upon the ground.

There were other minor damages around the city. Trees had been uprooted, signs were gone, one street was destroyed and a couple of the large statues of the Glorious Leader and the other heroes of the Racial War suffered some damages. There were several Tree Spiders that had been blown in by the storm that were searching for prey.

Colonel Gorski and Major Evart had immediately sent out the Marines and the Army to assist in damage repairs. The citizens were slowly coming out of their barricades to enter back into their lives. The soldiers were using laser rifles set on kill blast to combat the Tree Spider issue.

Fortunately, the Great Protective Wall surrounding Clovis City had not been damaged. If there had been any cracks or breaks, it would have given the flesh eating creatures outside the wall the opportunity to bust in. Colonel Gorski had ordered that the Engineer Corps make the wall their first priority. After the wall inspections had been completed, the engineers moved on to the water and solar cell supplies. The nuclear generators had been inspected and cleared by the planetary scientists under the supervision of Major Sigebert Evart.

All was well, except for the alert at the Cordell Hull United Nations Hospital. Over thirty men and women had been murdered by two men. One was restrained and had a tooth removed by Doctor Freya Doernitz Cardenas at the request of Frank Preston, a Military Intelligence operative. The second killer died when he fell on his own knife while fighting cadet Les Gillis. Lieutenant Simms had led the Army response to the alert and his platoon had secured the crime scene at the hospital. Criminal Investigation Division was already present, interviewing the witnesses and survivors.

Colonel Gorski had made it to his office early in the morning and Major Evart arrived moments after he had. They found that Sean Collins had been at work before them. He was present with three paralegals and another lawyer going through mounds of paperwork. The two Marine officers were accustomed to Collins beating them to the office as the lawyer kept long hours. But that morning, Collins had many of his legal staff working and in the office before everyone else. That could only mean that Collins was working on a case of significance. Colonel Gorski was curious as to the nature of the lawsuit or case that Collins was feverishly working on. He decided to be nosey and find out what had the director of all of the legal activity on New Edinburgh working so early. Gorski knocked on the door to Collins' huge, spacious office.

"Come in!" Collins called out loud.

Gorski entered the office, "I see you are very busy this morning counselor."

"Close the door," Collins instructed Colonel Gorski.

Collins waited until Gorski complied. "Have a seat." Normally Collins would wish one "good morning" or ask how they were doing this day. But today, he was not his normal courteous self. His mind was on about hundreds of different items, all of which needed to be completed yesterday. Gorski could see that Collins was in his environment, working a huge case, directing his staff and multi-tasking as only Collins could do.

Gorski sat in front of Collins desk. He saw a large twenty-four ounce cup of coffee on the desk and watched as Collins would take large drinks from it.

"Our plan worked," Collins finally told the Colonel. "Your son, his friends and your unit of stealth protectors caught three hit teams. They were sent in by the Rosenburg's to kidnap your son and some of his friends."

"What? Was my son involved?"" Gorski sat forward, surprised that this was the first he was hearing of such a thing. He had been made aware that the hospital had an incident during the late night hours, but he had not been brought any details or intelligence regarding the attack.

"Yes, Yuri was involved," Collins nodded. "He is fine. He actually fought so well, that he might qualify for some sort of medal."

"My own son gets into another fight for his life and

he doesn't bother to contact me?"

Collins shrugged, "I hear he said that he did not want to wake you up because you needed your beauty sleep."

Gorski laughed, "My son would say something like that."

"Well he is safe as are the other four cadets that were targets."

Gorski looked over at the staff in Collins office. "Don't talk about it so loud. Can you trust these other people?" Gorski was whispering and motioned to the other employees in his legal unit. "Was anyone hurt?"

Collins nodded, "Yes, unfortunately one of your men, Hodges, was killed. A few cadets were also killed and there were a few injuries. The hospital incident, which I am sure you heard about on the way to work, was the result of one of the hit teams. They were after Les Gillis and went wild, shooting people at random with new weapons that vaporized their victims. So all of those deaths were a part of last night's attack. And please do not worry about my staff, they are all professionals and will maintain strict confidentiality of all discussions and legal strategy."

"And they captured all of the assailants?" Gorski was hopeful. He made a mental note to see his son and apologize for not believing him.

"Yes," Collins affirmed. "Well, except for four of them. Two committed suicide by cyanide. One fell off a rooftop and another fell on his own knife. We have five under arrest. I am issuing an arrest warrant for another named co-conspirator on the space station. I will need you and your entire military prepared for defensive action. The ringleader is a big fish."

"How big?" Colonel Gorski inquired.

"The most powerful and wealthiest man on the planet, Alfred Rosenburg." Collins drank some more coffee, watching Gorski's face for a reaction. "It would seem that the Rosenburg Ranch is a big front for a massive human slave trade. I am going to file indictment requests with the Grand Jury this afternoon. I need some allies since this has the probability of getting nasty very quickly."

"Nasty? That is the understatement of the century. They are all related to the Glorious Leader. You make a move against the Rosenburg's then the Sikorsky Regime will certainly take some form of action."

"Nikolai, I have thought all about that. I have not slept since I was contacted about the ambush in the dormitories. We have to stand for something and we need to make that stand now. I became a lawyer to fight for justice and for the rights of the people. I will not be an idle bystander in life while the descendants of the Glorious Leader commit wanton acts of rape, murder and enslave others. I need you, Nikolai. I need Sigebert and the rest of the armed forced to back my play here. I have a few good prosecutors that are committed to this and we have a few honest judicial officers that will not be bribed or threatened. I need the military."

Gorski sighed and leaned back in his chair. Nasty and bloody, he thought to himself. The Rosenburg family was well connected. General Leta Tan, the commander of New Edinburgh planetary Military Intelligence, was a supporter of the Rosenburg's. They were descendants of the Glorious Leader and had promoted Tan to a rank that she probably had not deserved to receive. Tan was a general only because she did the bidding of the Royal Family without question, including executing civilians on the street for merely debating the laws. If Collins was going after the entire family, then Tan would not be in favor of such an action. If Vladimir Sikorsky stuck his nose into the issue, then things could get quite messy. Fortunately, Tan's base of operations was located on Lynott's Land and about two hundred miles away and Sikorsky was governing from another solar system.

Gorski also recalled the tragedy of Darktober in which several high ranking officers were killed by professional assassins. The Rosenburg's had always been suspected in that criminal investigation, but the CID never could positively link the family to the crime.

"Sean, you do remember Darktober?"

Collins glared at his friend for a second, "I lost my wife in that crossfire, Nikolai. No one remembers it more than me. I still have to hear some of my youngest ask when their mother will be coming home. Do you have any idea how difficult that is, to have to keep telling those sweet kids that they will never see their mother again?"

Gorski nodded, "I know Sean. I know. I went through it with Yuri when Melita died. I think we understand one another."

"So, will you help me do what needs to be done?"

"I will triple security for the building and assign escorts for you and your top prosecutors. I will also arrange for security for all of your family members, although Eamon O'Grady is more than capable of protecting your daughter Ginger. I will have around the clock security for the holding cells on the south side of Clovis City. What else do you need?" Gorski shifted in his seat.

Collins was thinking for a moment to find the best

way to ask before responding, "I need a safe house for a very special witness. No one but you and I can know where she is. She will need a few guards to watch over her. We will need your most trusted women and men to protect her. We cannot lose her."

Gorski was deep in thought regarding the request, "I think I have just the place."

Gorski watched Collins directing a female lawyer named Nia Li to prepare a motion and affidavit for business records on all of the Transport schedules from Space Station Cy-7. He then ordered a paralegal to re-write an indictment on some defendant that the Colonel had never heard of before. Gorski was amazed how the lawyer could keep so many names and facts in his head, direct so much traffic and still hold a conversation and work on his computer, typing like a man possessed. He stood up and decided he should alert Evart and a few of his most trusted officers to get ready to assist in the process. One witness needed a safe house and protection. Gorski and his Marines would gladly provide that service. Other criminal defendants would need to be transported to holding cells, which Gorski could arrange. Extra protection for Collins and his legal staff would be necessary as well. If the lawyer was really breaking open this case, as he seemed to certain of, then he would need to be watched.

Gorski also needed to address the more immediate issue of assignments of guards to his son's friends. They would need a replacement for Hodges to be sent to watch over Cadet Michel Evart.

Gorski excused himself from Collins office and walked back to his section down the long, winding hallway. He noticed that Rebecca Rosenburg, the personal advisor to Alexander Lyss, was watching the legal section. Gorski had long since concluded that the young woman was spying on everything. He made a mental note to keep an eye on her. She was one of the children of Alfred Rosenburg the Second. Accordingly, she could not be trusted. Gorski hoped that Collins had warned his staff to keep the woman out of the loop and keep the top secret documents from her.

Rebecca Rosenburg had made it to her office at seven in the morning. She was surprised to see that Collins and several of his most trusted legal staff already at work. Rebecca had been sent to work at the United Nations building by her father, to keep a close watch on Alexander Lyss and advocate for the interests of her family. Rebecca was wearing a tight black mini-skirt and a white blouse, with the top two buttons undone to show off her cleavage.

She had been taught by her family that sexual attraction was a powerful tool to gain information. She knew something big was going on. One of the younger lawyers that had been hired by Collins last year had been asking Rebecca out for a date for some time. She would always say she was too busy. It was time to tell him she was free. She needed to know all of the details of what all the activity was about.

Rebecca had prided herself on her ability to obtain information for her family. Since the prior evening, her father and mother had been contacting her every thirty minutes for any reports on the Ragnarsson assassin team. From what Rebecca had learned from her family, Junior Ragnarsson had failed to return to the Rosenburg Ranch. That fact had many of the Rosenburg's worried, and for good reason. Junior knew everything about their operations, specifically the illegal slave trade that they were operating out of the Rosenburg Ranch Territory. If Collins needed an excuse to send in investigators to breach the territorial integrity of the Rosenburg Ranch, an accusation of slaves being held there would form the perfect excuse to do so.

CHAPTER TWO

Like Rebecca, Penelope Rosenburg had been trying in vain to gain information regarding the fate of the Ragnarsson assassination team. In her mind, Penelope had been secretly hoping that the kind hearted Les Gillis and his friends would find a way to thwart the hired killers. She had reported to her office at the Baroness Hotel just after four in the morning, Clovis City time. She had five of the main satellite three dimensional news broadcasts on the western wall of her office playing simultaneously while she searched for information on her personal computer. She had attempted to contact Gillis via holo-com without success. That meant that Gillis was dead, captured or unable to respond. But she found that there was a fourth possibility.

She wondered if Colonel Gorski would have been astute enough to seek a court ordered blackout on the news reporters in Clovis City regarding the hit team. Penelope checked her theory and found that there was such a restraining order that had been filed and signed by one of the United Nations District judges. She read the name of the lawyer that filed the order.

"Sean Collins," Penelope whispered. "Well played. Well played."

She verbally ordered her office computer system to request a large vanilla caramel latte from the hotel room service staff as she continued her search for information.

As was her morning habit, Ella Ragnarsson had her cup of triple vanilla latte in her left hand as she approached the entrance to the Baroness Hotel on Space Station Cy-7. She was wearing a skin tight red dress which showed off her athletic body. Men would stop and stare at her as she walked by them. She smiled to herself, thinking no man could resist her. As she neared her place of employment she noticed that there were several men and women approaching her. One of the group that was closing in on her was the Criminal Investigation Division Chief Bennington. Several of the others were armed soldiers and Marines. She realized that they were not interested in small talk or a social visit. Something was up. She began to slow her pace some, not enough to be obvious.

"Ella Ragnarsson," Bennington said loudly. "I have a warrant for your arrest for the murder of Lieutenant Garrison, conspiracy for two counts of attempted rape, conspiracy for two counts of aggravated kidnaping, conspiracy for two counts of attempted murder, felony murder and conspiracy to destroy evidence after the fact. We have you surrounded so do not try and flee."

Ella stopped walking and she surveyed her options. She could flee to the hallway on her left if she could get past the soldiers blocking her way. Her route to the safety of the Baroness Security section was completely cut off by Bennington and his police. She knew that in a matter of seconds, more soldiers would surround her from behind, if they had not done so already. She watched as Bennington began walking toward her. She waited until he was just a few feet away and then threw her coffee at his face. She heard him scream as she ran to her left. She heard the laser shots behind her as she fled down the long corridor. She did not get far. She felt the electrical charge of the laser coursing through her body. She fell to the metal floor of the space station as she lost consciousness, wondering who had talked and why.

As the soldiers bound her legs and arms, several medical technicians appeared with a stretcher on wheels. They loaded the woman onto the rolling bed.

Bennington wiped the coffee from his face. It had been warm enough to sting, but not cause any burns. "Get her to the dental section. I want that molar removed ASAP."

An hour earlier, Bennington received the judicial document on his personalized encrypted computer mailbox from Sean Collins. It was marked "Top Secret" with an order for the immediate arrest and detention of Ella Ragnarsson at five in the morning. He had immediately assembled a team to carry out the order of the Judge and detain her. Bennington had read the indictment against the woman. In his heart, he realized he should have been more supportive of Garrison. The deceased chief of space station security had been right all along. The cadets had not lied.

The soldiers and medical personnel complied and wheeled Ella down the long halls of the space station.

From the Baroness Hotel, Penelope Rosenburg witnessed the arrest. She had wanted to help her friend Ella, but the numbers were not in their favor. As the soldiers carted Ella away, Penelope moved quickly to the safety of her offices. She was not running as she did not want to attract unwanted attention. She arrived to her office and ordered her computer to shut and secure the door.

"Computer, person to person, Alfred Rosenburg the Second," Penelope said, her voice was shaking due to her feeling nervous regarding the events that had transpired. Something had gone very wrong.

A three-dimensional view of Penelope's father

appeared before her. It was a life sized view. One of his wives, Magdalena, was standing next to him.

"What seems to be the problem? Do you have any idea what time it is?" Alfred demanded with an angry tone of voice. But the truth of the matter was that he was not angry about the time of the call. He was angry because he was waiting on a call from another daughter, Rebecca, so that he could learn how badly the Ragnarsson team that was sent in did.

Penelope swallowed. Her father never said things like "good morning" or "great to hear from you." He was always blunt and to the point.

"Father," Penelope began, uneasy that the heartless and cruel step-mother Magdalena was part of the conversation. "Something is wrong here. Ella Ragnarsson was just arrested by a couple of squads of military soldiers. She tried to run but they stunned her. What is happening?"

There was silence as Magdalena and Alfred whispered into each other's ears. Penelope waited for her father to answer her. The silence was unbearable to her. She needed answers. Did this arrest have something to do with Caine's idiocy? Was it some other past murder that Ella had been involved in?   Finally her father spoke, "I will get back with you. This is news to us. Do not contact me again. I will contact you."

The three-dimensional broadcast ceased at the Rosenburg Ranch source. Penelope slammed her fist on her desk in frustration. She could not take the not knowing. She prided herself on being on top of the information. She cursed in frustration.

Magdalena Rosenburg had a plate of cantaloupe and ate a bite. She watched as her husband, Alfred, sat down at their large, twenty-four seat, kitchen table. He had a cup of blended juices for his breakfast. Being over one hundred seventy years old meant Alfred had to consume foods that were healthier. This was even true given most of his internal organs were harvested from young teen-age girls. The rest were mechanical implants created by medical pioneers.

"Is there something you have not told me?" Alfred said with a tint of accusation in his voice. There were three slaves in the kitchen, doing various chores. When they heard his tone of voice, they immediately dispersed and left the room. They had seen random slaves gutted by Rosenburg in times when he was angry. He would lash out at any random slave and they had no desire to be his next victim.

Magdalena calmly placed her plate of cantaloupe

slices on the table. She pointed her fork at his direction, her eyes burning in anger. "Do you really think that I would do something behind your back? Everything I did was to protect Caine, you and this family. All of my actions were discussed with you in advance. You approved everything."

"What went wrong?" Alfred Rosenburg changed the point of Magdalena's anger. "Why is Ella being arrested?"

"I don't know, but I will find the answer soon," Magdalena promised. "And one of us needs to contact her father, Dell. He will not be thrilled with the news that his favorite daughter has been incarcerated."

Alfred sighed, realizing that she was correct. Dell would most likely be livid when he learned that one of his favorite children had been arrested. "The contact should be personal. If the authorities are on to us for some slip up, or because someone had loose lips, then they will be monitoring all of our out-going and in-coming transmissions. We would only give the law enforcement more information. Plus, Dell can be violent in his methods. I do not want him losing his cool and initiating something that might blow up in our faces."

Magdalena took a bite of cantaloupe. She recalled many years past in which Dell Ragnarsson lost a wife on a mission. She was killed by a body guard of a politician on the Martian Colonies. Dell, in his rage, tracked down the parents and children of the body guard and killed them all. Dell had been arrested while on Earth after killing the children of the guard. The Rosenburg's were forced to spend large sums of money and use their influence to convince the courts and the prosecutors to dismiss the matter and for the records to be electronically erased. Although he was the best of all assassins, he was capable of going off on unprofessional, personal vendettas. The man needed to be handled with care and kept in check. If any of his children had been harmed, he would want vengeance. But vengeance must be obtained in a manner that left plausible explanations to cover ones tracks. "I will check into what is happening," Magdalena assured Alfred. "If anyone should tell Dell anything, it should be me. We go way back and he trusts me. I will do it in person. He told me that he is on the other side of the solar system. If I call him in, he can be here within a few weeks. I, or someone else, should go to him and tell him any bad news in person. If he learns of any bad information on his own, he will come for retribution."

"You go," he waived his hand as if he were bored. "Let me know what you find out. And keep him from coming charging in for revenge. We need time to assess what happened, why it happened and then decide our best option to kill Gorski and his friends."

The kitchen door slid open and Carla Rosenburg, one of Alfred's daughters, was standing there. She was wearing tight gymnasium shorts, tennis shoes and a half shirt. Her blonde hair was tied into a pony tail. She wore an outfit did not hide her slender body, toned legs and firm breasts. Her face was lovely. Her father had been having an incestuous relationship with Carla for the past several years. It had started when Carla was just a young teenager. The physical nature of their father daughter relationship was a secret that they kept from the others. Some in the family gossiped about Carla because she was so attractive but never had a boyfriend around. The family did not realize that their father and Carla were secretly sleeping together.

"Father, I am worried. Rebecca contacted me from the U.N. Administrative Building. She said that the prosecution office has filed several indictments with the criminal courts. That damned Collins is coming after all of us," Carla announced as her father was checking out her figure. She smiled since it had been several days since father shared her bed.

"So?" He was curious as to why that fact would

concern Rebecca and Carla both.

"You were indicted," Carla told him. "So were Mr. Ragnarsson and most of his children. Some of my brothers and sisters were also named. They are accusing you of murder, father, and they know about all of the slaves here on the Ranch. They also indicted half of my brothers and sisters."

Alfred began breathing heavily as he lost control of his temper. Collins was an insolent plebeian and had no right to challenge him or any of the Royal Family for that matter. He stood up and grabbed a large ten inch bladed knife. He walked out of the kitchen without a word and into the large den and found a young woman there, a slave from a family in India. She was cleaning the bookshelves and was being cautious in how she handled the books due to their age that were hundreds of years old. She saw Alfred walking toward her and was questioning why the family leader would be coming in her direction. Then, too late for her to flee, she saw the knife. She screamed and tried to turn and run, but he was on her, slashing her arms and forcing her to the ground. He pinned her to the floor with his legs on her arms, ripped open her slave clothing and slashed off her right breast. The woman screamed and begged as he kept slashing and stabbing her. He cut her neck and placed his open mouth on the wound, swallowing her warm blood. He had learned to love the taste of blood over the decades.

When her screams and struggles stopped, he stood and dropped the bloody knife onto the floor. A pool of blood was growing around the woman's body. Alfred was still breathing heavily and had a large amount of blood on his cheeks and chin, dripping down onto the floor.

"Feel better?" Magdalena challenged him. "Why do you insist on killing the staff? Do you have any idea how long it took to train her?"

"I don't care!" He yelled with blood dripping down his chin. "Find out why I have an indictment out for me! Do it or you end up like this worthless bitch on the floor!"

He stormed up the steps. Carla wanted to follow her father up the stairs because she knew that when he was angry his sex drive increased. But with Magdalena watching, Carla knew following him could be a mistake. Magdalena was an astute woman and watched everything closely. If she saw her follow her father then it might make Magdalena suspicious.

Magdalena called up to Alfred, "When I find out the information you wish to know, then what?"

"Kill everyone!" he responded.

Magdalena looked at Carla for a few moments, thinking. "Assemble some of your siblings and tell them that we have work to do. I want all of the human slaves moved to the catacombs. Replace them with the alien slaves. When the police, MI and the militzia show up, and they will very soon, I want them to leave with their tails between their legs."

Carla was looking at the dead body on the floor as Magdalena spoke to her. Father was not sound of mind, she thought. He would lose his temper often and it seemed to occur more frequently now. She momentarily put out of her mind the issues with her father and nodded to Magdalena. Carla knew Magdalena was correct in that the slaves must not be discovered. If they were, the prosecutors would indict the entire family. Everyone would potentially be arrested and sent away for a long time. The family had bought off judges and prosecutors in the years past. But, according to Rebecca, Collins was too honorable a man. He could not be bribed or intimidated and he would not stop until he got justice for the victims. He would pursue this case to the bitter end. That thought scared Carla as she was not accustomed to men that were incorruptible. She had no desire to spend the rest of her life growing old while incarcerated on planet Cootron.

CHAPTER THREE

The news media had been kept in the dark by the military at the dormitories ever since the gag order had been issued by the district judge. Sean Collins and his legal team were leaving nothing to chance. All of the satellite systems over planet New Edinburgh were temporarily taken off-line so that the Rosenburg family would not be able to obtain the information regarding the failures of Junior Ragnarsson and his team.

Ivar Ragnarsson was taken in chains along with his sister-in-law Dulce by the platoon of Marines under the command of Lieutenant Price.

Jen Staszko, Elektra Papanikolaou, LaShondra Lewis and Sara Stewart watched in silence as the two were taken away. The Marines had placed dark hoods on the heads of the two and similar hoods on five other decoys so that any snipers or would be assassins could not be able to tell who was who. The entire spectacle had been carefully arranged by the prosecution team assembled by Collins. Dulce Ragnarsson had been instructed step by step what to expect. She would be taken as if she were under arrest and then moved to a secure location. She understood that there was a great chance she would not survive the events. The Ragnarsson's and Rosenburg's had spies everywhere, but it was worth the risk to her. If this man Collins could put an end to the terror of the two families, then the sacrifice would merit the effort.

The two prisoners were loaded onto separate large metal transport ships and guided down in seats as they could not see with the hoods covering their eyes. There were seven transports in total and each received a person in a hood. This was a ploy to throw off any on-lookers with interest in tracking down the location of the informant. The other five men in hoods were "decoys." The seven ships lifted off the pavement and began flying up into the sky in different directions.

After a few minutes in flight, Dulce Ragnarsson felt her hood and handcuffs being removed. She opened her eyes and saw the lawyer Sean Collins sitting in front of her.

"How are you doing so far?" Collins asked her.

She smiled when she recognized the man and leaned across the aisle and hugged the man. "My personal hero," she said with glee. "I have never been better. I feel like I am free."

"And we are going to work very hard at keeping it that way," Collins promised her. "Arrests are being made as we speak."

"Have you arrested Ella or Dell Ragnarsson yet?" Dulce asked with dread in her voice.

Collins kept his voice calm and soothing as he responded, "We got Ella this morning. She tossed her coffee at the arresting officers and they had to stun her. Dell is unaccounted for. We have no idea where he is."

"He was not in our solar system as of yesterday," Dulce said softly. "But when he learns that his sons and daughters are incarcerated, he will come. People are going to die. You understand what a risk you are taking with this case? He is very dangerous."

Collins had already considered everything. He and his family were being guarded; the United Nations Building was on high alert. The military had been put on notice. Even with the additional precautions, Collins understood that Dell Ragnarsson was a man of means. He was capable of taking action, regardless of the odds he faced. Even with the danger posed in the matter, Collins and his legal staff had come to a consensus that they would not allow the citizens of New Edinburgh to be intimidated or threatened any longer.

It was time to take a stand.

Jen Staszko and the others walked back into their dormitory, each of them exhausted from the night without sleep. Colonel Gorski had instructed their personal guards to stay with them until further notice.

"I feel like we have all been vindicated somehow," Elektra said as she watched the seven transports shooting off into the sky. "If some convictions come of this, will we all be safe again?"

"I don't know," Staszko shrugged. "You know what would be really good right now - Pancakes, biscuits, sausage links, lots of syrup, a bowl of strawberries and a bottomless cup of coffee. Who is with me?"

The three women nodded in agreement and followed Staszko toward the cafeteria. They were all starving.

Staszko leaned into her friend Elektra, "How am I going to get any alone time with Yuri if these two stay on our tails?"

Elektra thought for a moment, "Just let them watch?"

"You mean let the soldiers watch?" Staszko scowled

at that remark. She liked the younger cadet from Greece, but could not understand her sense of humor sometimes.

Lewis caught up to the two women; Stewart was behind them watching the rear.

"So, ladies, I thought we should make arrangements for you two to have some alone time with your significant others. Jen, I know you and Gorski are involved. But Elektra here, I don't know much about your man. Who is he?"

Elektra pondered the question, "I have been alone for some time. But Arch recently got my attention and I think I would like to see him on a more serious level."

"And do you two know any men for Sara and me?" Lewis asked.

Staszko stopped and looked at Stewart, "I think Drew would like her a lot."

"And me?" Lewis asked.

"With your smile and body? There are dozens that would like you," Staszko concluded. "Tell me what kind of man you like, and I will make it happen. Anything for my new best friend."

Lewis laughed, "I really like this assignment."

The mood at the Cordell Hull Hospital was one of sadness. Several staff lost their lives in the attack of the night before. Most of the security guards had died. Doctor Harding and Doctor Doernitz Cardenas had been working overtime to help keep the calm and assist the Marines and investigators to sort out the tragedy.

Lester Brey Gillis had spent two hours being interviewed by members of the Clovis City Militzia and the military Criminal Investigation Division. He had not slept all night as he, Julia Steiner, Preston, and others gave a hand to assist the hospital staff with the patients. Gillis grew weary of the constant questions regarding the death of Prescott. After the grueling questioning had ended, Gillis gave an electronic signature on his statement to the authorities and was released. He waited in the lobby for his shadow, Preston, to join him.

Steiner was also there, rubbing her eyelids with her fingertips. She was clearly exhausted, fighting the urge to put her head down and sleep. She smiled at Gillis when she saw him sit next to her. "I feel horrible."

"Me too," Gillis said. "You did great."

"You too," Steiner said and took hold of his hand. "I never shot an actual person before."

"You did it like a professional," Gillis affirmed. "And I hear you did a good job assisting on the removal of Nikko's suicide pill."

"That was really tricky. One slip up and we would have ruptured the capsule. Please tell me that cretin will go to jail for a long time."

"He may even receive the death penalty," Gillis observed, repeating something he heard from one of the MI officers. "If he cooperates and names some names, he might only get a few stacked life sentences." He stretched his arms over his head and yawned. "Don't worry, he won't be back."

"I was told I may have to testify in court," Steiner also stretched as she spoke. "How did we get in the middle of this, Les?"

"I was in the right place at the wrong time. If I had been there earlier, I could have saved Dray. At least we stopped them from harming Elektra any more than they did. This whole situation is like a nightmare. I have been in touch with Jen and Yuri and they were also attacked."

"What?" Steiner sat up, suddenly feeling some energy. "Three attacks at once? That really took some serious planning and coordination. Are the others safe?"

Gillis nodded, "Yes, for the most part. Klaus broke both of his arms in a fall down the staircase. He is being rushed over here as we speak. Two cadets in the science department were killed, I did not know them. Will Bragg was killed. With Amir and Dray dead, it feels like open season on all of us. These weren't average men and women. These were professionals. We just got very lucky that the list of victims was low."

Steiner was silent, pondering the words of her friend. She watched emergency medical technicians rush in some victims from the dust storm and the dormitory attacks. Many people had suffered some minor injuries during the sand storm. One of the new patients arriving was Klaus Rhinehard. He was being brought in on a wheeled stretcher with his brother, Rolf, and April Mejia close behind. Steiner stood when she saw them enter and covered her mouth with her hands.

Steiner noticed that Mejia had redness in her eyes. She approached her friend and hugged her. "April, I am so sorry. Have they said how he is?"

"They think they can set his arms with some metal support plates," Mejia told her. "They say he will be able to fly again in a few months. I was so scared." She started sobbing again, clinging to Steiner. "I love him so much. I thought I was going to lose him."

Steiner held her close, "It's going to be okay. He is alive, he is strong and there was no permanent damage. You just take good care of him."

Mejia only nodded to Steiner's words. Mejia had always kept in contact with Steiner, even though she had left the group. Mejia had confided in her that she and Klaus had become lovers. Steiner always had a suspicion that Mejia and Klaus would one day be together as she had observed how Klaus could never seem to take his eyes off of Mejia. It was a good match, Steiner thought to herself.

Rolf sat down and put his head in his hands. He worried for his older brother. Klaus had always watched over him and Rolf never had considered the possibility of losing Klaus. The knowledge that his brother could have suffered worse injuries shook Rolf to the bone. He felt Gillis' hand on his shoulder.

"You okay, kid?"

"Yes," Rolf answered quickly and then frowned. "No. I am not sure. They say Klaus will be fine." The truth was that Rolf felt numb. His older brother was his closest sibling and he could not fathom what life would be like without him. Yesenia Guevara had given a statement to the authorities. She spent over an hour answering questions from CID, local police and Lieutenant May Ling from the Military Intelligence section. After Guevara completed the interviews, she entered the lobby and saw Steiner, Mejia, Gillis and Rolf. The sight of her friends brought a smile to her face. It was a partial Gorski Gang reunion in progress. Guevara said hello to each and every one of those assembled before her. She eventually made her excuses so that she could return home. Guevara had her son in her arms and he was hungry. She wanted to get him home to feed him. With her husband dead she had only her son now. It was going to take some time for her to adjust to a new way of living. The best part was she no longer had to be in fear of the physical violence of her husband. She was surprised at herself in that she did not miss William Bragg at all.

Nikko woke up in a hospital bed with his left hand bound by plastic straps to the metal bed post. His mouth felt numb and his head was throbbing. He was immediately aware that someone had surgically removed his suicide pill. He inspected his room and quickly memorized the exact location of the windows and the doors. There was an empty bed to his right. To his left was a window where there was ample daylight coming through. There were muffled voices outside of his room. Nikko was angry at himself for letting the situation get so out of control. Prescott had always been an idiot, but this time he had exceeded his highest levels of being unprofessional. With over thirty deaths to their names, he was cognizant of what would happen next. Some prosecutor would try and cut him a deal to sell out Dell Ragnarsson. Turning over any form of evidence against the Ragnarsson family would be a death sentence and, therefore, Nikko would refuse to cooperate. The prosecution would then file indictments against Nikko and obtain multiple felony convictions against him. He wished he had just taken his suicide pill. It was far too late now and he would have to face the consequences.

An attractive female doctor entered his room. Her name tag read "Cardenas." She checked his pulse without showing any emotion. "He is awake," Freya Cardenas announced loudly.

A Marine officer entered the room, his rank insignia indicated he was a Major and his name tag read "Evart." He was wearing the war class uniform, a long sleeved one piece with random patterns of black, green and brown and a zipper in the front that went half way down the torso. He had a utility belt around his waist with a laser pistol, twelve inch knife, his hand held holo-com device and some pouches with items unknown to Nikko. His boots were black.

Evart had a plain-clothed detective with him.

"Good morning, sir. I am Major Sigebert Evart. Forgive me if I refuse to shake your hand, but you and your friends tried to kidnap my nephew last night." Evart sat down on the stool next to Nikko's bed. "We do know your name and we know who you work with. You see, another of your team, an Emma Ragnarsson, sang like a canary."

Nikko said nothing. He knew that the police lied about cases. They would ad lib information to coerce confessions. Police were not to be trusted. But, a Major in the Marines would be different. The Marines were one of the few branches of the military that had honor. In addition, Nikko noticed a young Asian female wearing the solid black uniform of the Military Intelligence Branch standing in the doorway. Her shoulders had the gold bar signifying that she was a Second Lieutenant. The woman said nothing but was listening intently to the conversation between the Major and Nikko.

Major Evart continued as Doctor Cardenas excused herself from the room. "We know about Ella. You should know that we just arrested her. We know about Dell Ragnarsson and his son, who was your team leader. Junior is also under arrest. His father has about five hundred indictments signed by the Judge as of this morning. Warrants for his arrest have been issued in all Earth planetary systems. We also will be rounding up the family members of the Rosenburg's for murder for hire and slavery. Your man Prescott is dead. Dulce is dead. Chang and Montrose are dead. I wanted to give you the chance to give us some more details before you are sent to the Tank."

Nikko was silent, fully aware that remaining quiet could net him a death penalty finding. Talking would bring certain death from Dell Ragnarsson. Nikko was confident that no matter how many indictments or arrest warrants that the law enforcement issued, they would never catch Dell Ragnarsson. He was far too crafty for the police or the military. Nikko elected to remain silent.

A few minutes passed as Evart watched Nikko. The Marine Corps officer finally determined that Nikko would not speak.

"Take him to the Tank!" Evart barked.

Several uniformed Marines came into the room and wheeled the assassin out of the hospital room. Nikko did not fight as he was taken away. His only hope now was for Dell Ragnarsson to rescue him and the rest of the team.

Evart smiled at the other officer, Lieutenant May Ling. "Tell General Tan how grateful we are that she was able to spare some of you to assist us in this."

Ling smiled back at him, "The pleasure is ours, Major. General Tan always stands ready to cooperate with the other military sections."

Evart walked out of the room with Ling following. Evart was concerned about getting general Tan involved as her methods were far more brutal than Colonel Gorski's. Evart wondered if Lieutenant Ling was one of General Tan's many lovers. The General had a reputation for surrounding herself with female officers that she could manipulate to perform sexual acts with her. It was well known that Tan would only draft and recruit females for officer positions in her unit. Evart had never visited the Military Intelligence base of operations located in Lynott's Land. He speculated in his mind that the buildings were akin to the mythical Amazons, all women and no men.

Doctor Freya Doernitz Cardenas had finished the busiest shift of her life. There were several emergency room admissions due to the deadly dust storm that had passed through the city and all she could think about was that she needed to sit down and relax, for just a moment.

Freya had already been on her feet for approximately twenty hours non-stop. She had to go to the restroom in a bad way. As she was walking toward the ladies room, she heard the yells of joy from behind her. It was the voices of her children, Alejandro and Maria. Freya turned to see her two children running toward her at full steam.

"Mommy! Mommy!" Alejandro kept repeating.

Maria was also screaming with glee, "Momma!"

The two children had their arms held out in front of them, in anticipation of the inevitable bear hug they would receive from their mother. Freya did not disappoint them. She knelt down on her knees and her children fell into her arms, and held her close. For a moment, she forgot how tired she was.

"Mommy loves you both so much!" She told her children. There were a few moments during the siege at the Hospital that she believed she would never see her children again. She felt her mortality up front and personal. The men that had attacked were immoral and godless, they killed without reason. She prayed often during the night, that the Lord would protect the rest of the hospital staff and patrons. Her prayers had been answered by the brave actions of Les Gillis, Julia Steiner and the man named Preston.

"Honey, we heard what happened and rushed over as soon as we were told," Freya heard her husband's voice, cadet Porfirio Cardenas. She stood up, holding both children, one in either arm. Her husband kissed her on the lips. Freya saw that her brother Jurgen Doernitz was also there. He kissed her on the cheek.

"We were really worried," Jurgen told his sister.

"Te quiero mucho. I love you." Porfirio kissed her some more.

"I love you too," Freya told her husband between kisses. She thanked God for the moment. Her family was safe and the men with the evil in their hearts were either dead or under arrest. She felt the glow of the New Edinburgh red-orange color flowing into the hospital corridor. God willing today would be a great day.

Sergeant First Class Mark Lund had turned Junior Ragnarsson and Quintana over to the platoon of Marines that had arrived at the Men's Dormitory. Yuri Gorski, Drew Harrison and Michel Evart stood by and observed the transfer. Both of the would-be kidnappers had their suicide pills removed from their teeth by cadets Blundell and Windfohr. Every precaution was being taken to insure that there would be no escape.

Two marines had hold of Junior Ragnarsson's arms as they escorted him toward one of the military transport space craft. He turned his head and faced Yuri Gorski. Junior had never lost before and the situation angered him. He had walked into an ambush that was orchestrated by amateurs. No, he had been lured; tempted into the waiting trap that Gorski and his friends had planned. Junior was not certain as to whether he was angrier at Gorski or himself.

"You little shit's think you won. Think again. You and Evart are dead men walking. Harrison, you fucked yourself by getting involved. You are all dead. Enjoy the small amount of time you have left on this purple planet. You will all die, and I will walk out of jail with a dismissal and the Judge begging my forgiveness." Junior told the cadets with joy in his voice. "When you least expect it, expect it. When we come for you, we may be dressed as nuns or missionaries. I might even come dressed up as you mother after I rape her and gut her. You will think that I am your own dead bitch mother before I kill you."

Yuri Gorski balled up his fist and hit Junior in the face. His face snapped backwards, his bottom lip busted and blood began to pour down his cheek.

"You ever insult my mother again and you will be the dead man walking," Gorski promised him. "Take him out of my sight."

Quintana said nothing as he walked with the Marines escorting him. They two prisoners were placed in separate military transport ships. Quintana sat in silence as he was chained to a metal bunk bed in one of the bottom rooms of his ship. Within a few minutes, he felt his ship lifting into the air. He had refused to speak when interrogated at the dormitory. He had gone into a rage when Gorski and Harrison had him injected with the truth serum. Once the drugs took over his resistance, he had confessed to every detail of his involvement. He felt ashamed that he was not strong enough to fight the effects of the injection. In addition, he had told his interrogators everything that he knew about the Ragnarsson assassin teams. Although his knowledge of the Rosenburg family was slim to none, Quintana was unable to avoid providing that information to the CID and MI questioners.

There were several criminal investigation undercover officers, Clovis City Militzia and Marines scouring the building and the outside pavement. Quintana had been told that pieces of Montrose had been found, here and there. He was also informed that Chang had taken his own life which grieved him. Quintana had regarded Chang as his closest friend and would miss his company.

Junior was forced down into a seat and cuffed to the metal bar that acted as an arm rest. The leader of the assassin team had also been interrogated while under the control of the truth serum. He had given the law enforcement and military officers details of his father and the Rosenburg family. He lamented the fact that he had failed his mission but his true sorrow was in the knowledge that he had betrayed his father and the clients. With the information extracted from him, the MI soldiers would be able to arrest virtually all of the Rosenburg's. His father would most likely be named the most wanted man in the galaxy.

A sergeant and three privates sat in the row of seats across from him. The three privates had fear in their eyes. All of the Marines had been briefed on the small portions of information regarding the assassins that was available. Many of the younger Marines were intimidated and even frightened by the tales of the numerous victims that suffered creeping death at the hands of the Ragnarsson's.

"Boo!" Junior said loudly. The three privates jumped at that as they were intimidated by him, scared even. Junior began to develop a plan so that he could use the situation to his advantage.

The four Marines were wearing their war uniforms. Junior noted that all of the Marines on board seemed to be armed with their issued hand lasers. They each also had the standard knife with a twelve inch blade. Each had two or more pouches on their utility belts. He surmised that the pouches had stun darts, flame darts or some explosive devices.

"You four, if you want to live long lives, better

listen close to what I have to tell you," Junior said as the Transport ship began to lift off. "My family has money, lots of money and unlimited resources."

"Pay no attention to him. He is a liar and a criminal!" The sergeant told the three privates.

Junior looked to his left and right. There were only a few other marines on the Transport ship. He estimated that meant there was a squad of eleven on board and a pilot, perhaps a co-pilot. That meant that there were at least thirteen men and women assigned to guard him. He looked back at the Sergeant and his three men.

"My father is a cruel man, but he is also very generous," Junior said so only the four of them could hear. He looked at their name tags. The Sergeant was named Gazepov. The three privates were Kulevska, Trevizo and Chretien. "How much do you lads make in a month? You set me free and my father will pay you ten, no one hundred times your current salaries."

"Don't listen. He is a liar!" Sergeant Gazepov growled at his men.

Junior smiled, "And, if you set me free, my father will allow you to live. If I go to jail, I will have my father track you down and kill you, your wives, your children, your dog, your cat and your birds and rats. Set me free, no one dies and you will be richly rewarded. You see, I know more about the four of you then you know about yourselves. Since the four of you are enlisted men in the service, you were all raised in orphanages. Neither one of you know who your birth parents were because they were peasants that could not even purchase a pot to piss in. Since each of you are in your current status, then I am deducing that neither of you were ever adopted and you probably spent seventeen miserable years in that orphan home being beaten or raped or both and when you were not being victimized, you spent your spare moments avoiding the abuse. Am I right?"

"How do you know so much about me?" Chretien blurted out.

"Stow it, Private!" Gazepov ordered. "He is only screwing with you. Don't listen to him."

Junior laughed, "Right. Don't listen to me. Why would I be any more honest than those bastards that mistreated you all as children and teens? I bet some of you have scars on your bodies from the years of physical assaults that you endured by your former caretakers. But I want to know is why are you loyal to the people that allowed that mistreatment to occur? No one from authority stepped up and saved you. All of you suffered and no body helped you. And those are the very same people, the very same infrastructure, and the very same hierarchy that you each serve now. They screwed you as children and they are continuing to do so by making you enforce their laws. The same laws that failed to protect each of you as children I might add. So, do as you wish. I offer you a chance at riches and a lifetime filled with beautiful naked women. The system will force each of you to continue to place innocent children into one of those homes. Ask yourselves, how would you be able to sleep at night if you placed a child in one of those homes? One day they will order you to do it. Now, if you want to avoid that eventuality, join with me. Release me and together we can travel the galaxy, kill a few fat pigs for big pay days and you will have more than you ever dreamed possible."

The four men said nothing.

"Okay," He sighed. "Tell me what it would take to get one of you to set me free. If one of you won't do it, send down one of your other squad members so I can negotiate with them. I have a ton of money to hand out. First one to act gets paid, laid and taken care of. The rest die badly."

The silence continued. Rough crowd, he thought to himself. He decided that he would need to find another way to escape. He would bide his time and pick the correct moment. Junior knew all about the model of military transport he was on. They were all as long as one hundred yards, eighty feet wide and sixty feet in height. They all had the same color schemes. The ships had ample fire power. Although the speed on the military transport ships was not the best, this ship would do well as a vehicle to escape in. He began to make his plans for escape.

"Fine, you won't help me," Junior shrugged as he looked around the hull and the floors of the ship. "Very noble of the four of you. The least you could do is tell me where we are going."

Sergeant Gazepov mulled the request over in his mind. He did not think that there would be any harm in telling the prisoner what his fate was to be. "You are being taken to the Southern Holding Cells. No person has ever escaped from there. Even if you did get out of the facility, which has underground cells and an impossible set of obstacles to get to the planet surface, you would have to avoid thousands of kilometers of the dinosaurs on the surface to get to another Territory. You will be held there until your trial date. After your sentence is pronounced, you will be sent to Cootron, the prison planet, and executed."

"Sentenced? Executed?" Junior was laughing at the

absurdity of the thought. "My dear Sergeant Gazepov, I will never even be tried in court. The charges against me will be dismissed. There will be no trial. You see, I am untouchable. I have friends in some of the most influential circles of life. I am the right hand of power, my friend. There will be no trial, no conviction, and no sentence. I will be free and that lawyer and the rest of you will all be dead."

As he was speaking, Junior was slowly pulling back his right hand index fingernail. While the Marines had searched him thoroughly, they had not thought to investigate into whether he had any mechanical limbs. Years ago, his father had him undergo a few medical procedures, to implant certain devices to assist, in case there would ever be an event that he would be captured. He had underneath his fake fingernails many items at his disposal. Under his right hand index finger were some gas pellets. He was immune to the gas as he had been inoculated against the gas each year. The gas would render any within a fifteen foot radius unconscious.

Junior had calculated in his mind how long they had been airborne. He knew by now they would no longer be over Clovis City Territory. They would be over the colorful forests of the planet New Edinburgh. Below would be the flesh eating monsters that the populace referred to simplistically as dinosaurs. He would release the gas pellets and then steal a knife from one of the unconscious soldiers to cut the bindings and set himself free. Taking the transport ship would be easy. The pilots would be occupied flying the vessel and unable to mount any serious defense. The rest of the squad would be taken off guard, not suspecting that their prisoner could escape so easily.

Before Junior dropped the gas pellets, he watched as Private Chretien stood up and stretched. Chretien then drew his laser pistol, aimed, fired a short orange-yellow colored burst and stunned Sergeant Gazepov. Privates Kulevska and Trevizo were smiling as their squad leader collapsed to the metal floor.

"Cut him free," Chretien told the other two Privates.

Junior smiled as Kulevska and Trevizo took off his bindings.

"You were correct about us, sir," Trevizo told him. "We were all orphans except for the sergeant. We were all three treated like we had no value in life whatsoever. So, we would like to roll with you instead."

"Very smart move, gentlemen. Now what is your next trick?" Junior asked them.

"Now, we take control of the ship so that we can drop you off somewhere safe and you can wire us the money you promised us," Chretien told him. "Bind the sergeant and give Mister Ragnarsson his weapons."

Junior gladly took possession of Gazebo's utility belt and put it around his own waist. He drew the laser pistol as he watched as Gazepov was handcuffed to the security bars. Trevizo gagged the sergeant, in case he woke up.

"Should we kill him?" Chretien asked while pointing at Gazepov.

"No, we are not barbarians," Junior responded. "He can live to tell the tale that a Ragnarsson cannot be held. Ever."

"You are the boss," Trevizo shrugged.

"So, what was it that made the three of you decide to betray your uniform and join up with me?" Junior was curious as to their motivation.

"Have any idea what they pay Private's today?" Chretien said. "It is peanuts. Plus, all three of us had been cadets at the Tyr Academy. We all three were busted out and forced into the enlisted ranks. All I did was slap a bitch for refusing to sleep with me. My sentence into this hell was unfair, even if the bitch was one of my professors."

"And what did you do to deserve being kicked out of the Academy and impressed into the military ranks?"

Junior asked as he was checking the utility pouches and found stun darts, flame darts and thermite grenades.

Trevizo smiled, "I was sleeping with the Dean's daughter and got her pregnant. The dean trumped up some false charges on me, claimed I was failing classes. I was booted out and ended up a Private. So, to hell with authority."

Junior laughed. He already liked this man. "Well, each of you will be well compensated. Lead on."

Chretien took point and led them up the hallway. He held up his hand in a fist to stop them after about fifty paces. Junior watched as Chretien drew his laser. Trevizo and Kulevska did the same. The three privates then moved quickly and began firing their lasers. Junior followed, ready for action. When he inspected the scene there were seven Marines on the floor, stunned. Chretien, Kulevska and Trevizo were securing the men and taking their utility belts.

"So far, so good," Junior said to himself. It was almost too easy. "How many left on board?"

"The two pilots," Trevizo was pointing upwards to the flight officer's command.

Junior followed the three mutineers and they made it to the flight module without incident. The two female pilots were laughing and telling each other jokes, unaware that they were being betrayed. Both pilots were wearing the standard issued dark blue, long sleeved, one piece, flight suit of the United Nations Space Command. One of the women was a Lieutenant and the other a Lieutenant Commander. Trevizo and Chretien stunned the two female officers and they both slumped forward in their flight chairs. The Lieutenant hit her head on the computerized control panel before her.

"Any of you know how to fly this thing?" Junior asked the men. He knew how, but he wanted to see what his three new men were made of.

Chretien and Trevizo moved the pilots out of their chairs and took their places. Kulevska bound the two pilot's hands and arms with plastic handcuffs. Junior watched with interest as the two privates took command of the flight controls. Chretien took the steering mechanism into his hands.

"Where to?" Trevizo asked Ragnarsson.

Junior stepped into the flight command capsule. He looked over the navigation command board to determine their exact location. He smiled as he realized where they were. "Eighty degree turn to the right, which should get us to Lynott's Territory."

"What will we do there?" Chretien asked.

"We will drop off this ship and the crew at a safe location," Junior informed them. "We will show the world that we are merciful by delivering them all alive. Then, we take a ship I own that is waiting for us on Lynott's Territory. After that we will be going to start a jail break."

"And when do we get paid?" Chretien wanted to know.

"As soon as we arrive in Lynott's Land. But, if you are interested in a lot more coin, then I suggest you make plans to come with me for a quick hit and run mission. I will pay you each fifty thousand. Interested?"

"Who is in jail that we are going to break out?" Kulevska asked him.

"My sister."

"Sounds great," Trevizo said.

CHAPTER FOUR

Penelope Rosenburg knew that things were going from bad to worse. She was speaking with her room service manager when the Baroness Hotel computer system alerted her that she had a set of visitors. The computer named her as "Smith," which was her assumed name. She politely excused herself from the meeting she was attending and walked to the front of the Hotel. She found that her "visitors" as the computer called them, were a crew of soldiers and criminal investigation division detectives, led by Bennington.

"Chief Bennington," Penelope stated and shook his hand, maintaining a professional demeanor. She noted that Bennington was wearing dark cargo pants, boots and a navy blue turtle neck sweater. He had a gun belt that held his hand laser, hand held holo-com device and two utility pouches.

She inspected the men and women with Bennington. She observed that many of the plain clothes detectives had disc recording devices, large back packs, lasers, and forensic packets. All of them were wearing protective plastic gloves. She noted that two of the male investigators were staring at her breasts. There were a few female detectives that were holding black briefcases in their hands filled with chemicals to detect blood, saliva, finger prints, DNA and other possible evidence. There was a young female Military Intelligence Lieutenant behind the group with a large gymnasium bag that contained empty evidence bags.

Bennington handed her a stack of papers, "We have search warrants for your entire hotel. We will do our best to not disturb your guests. But we expect complete cooperation from you and your staff."

"I do not understand," Penelope told him while reading quickly over the papers. Everything seemed legal, but she was not a lawyer. In her mind she knew this action was somehow connected with Ella's arrest. "What is it you expect to find?"

"First of all, that is none of your business. We will let you know when we find it," Bennington told her. "We need complete access to the entire hotel computer bank. Tell your employees if they do not cooperate I will have them arrested on the spot. That includes you ma'am."

Penelope nodded that she understood, "Follow me."

She knew her father would be extremely angry. If they were searching the Baroness, then certainly the next step would be the Rosenburg Ranch. She hoped her father had taken some protective action. She led the men into the security access area of the hotel. As they were walking, Penelope saw some of Bennington's officers using black lights, shining them on the floors and walls. She wondered what the detectives were searching for.

"Sir!" Detective Papalbon yelled. "We found blood traces."

Bennington looked in the direction where Papalbon was pointing and saw the white illumination of the stains of blood spatter. There were several up and down the hallway.

Penelope swallowed hard and hoped she was not turning red with anger toward her family. Ella had assured her that all of the trace blood evidence had been eliminated. Clearly the assurances were wrong.

"Scan the blood for DNA match," Bennington ordered.

Penelope watched as Papalbon pulled out another

instrument, a seven inch long and three inch wide DNA computerized scanner from the Allen Corporation. Papalbon leaned over the white droplets and began scanning the blood stains.

"Sir," Papalbon stated excitedly. "I am picking up two sets of DNA. I have uploaded the scans to the main computer. Hopefully we will have a match soon."

Bennington turned and faced Penelope, "Ma'am, what do you know of your security chief, Ella Ragnarsson?"

Penelope did her best to remain calm in the face of adversity, breathing normally and hoping that her face was not flush from her hidden anger. "Well, she was already working in her position when I was hired on as the hotel manager. She seemed capable and competent, she was knowledgeable. She showed up on time, worked late and had no disciplinary problems."

"Any family?"

"None that I ever met," Penelope lied. "What is going on here detective?"

Bennington pointed back down the hallway where Papalbon and others were still scanning. "I think we just found DNA evidence of the killers of Drayton Love-Easter. Now that we have this evidence, it is only a matter of time before the crime is solved."

Penelope cursed her half-brother Caine in her mind. The family was about to have some major problems. She recalled that Caine and his mentally unstable friends dragged the bleeding Darryl Rosenburg down the very hallway Papalbon was scanning. She already knew what the DNA scans would report. The blood could only belong to one person and that was Darryl.

"I have some work to complete," Penelope told Bennington. "May I be excused?"

Bennington looked the woman over, "Yes, but do not leave the space station until further notice. We will have to conduct a full interview with you later. Consider yourself on house arrest until further notice."

Penelope nodded at his instructions. She walked away from the investigation team toward her office and locked herself inside. She was ready to kill Caine herself. She tossed one of the visitor chairs across the room and screamed with rage. She slowly sat down behind her desk and began to control her breathing. She straightened her hair and spent about five minutes regaining her composure.

She decided she was ready to report to her family that the walls were closing in on them all. "Computer, person to person, attorney Alfred Rosenburg the Third on

Clovis City, planet New Edinburgh. Quickly."

It was not a normal day at the law firm of Alfred Rosenburg, III, and Ellis Ragnarsson. Both men had been personally contacted by investigators with the military Criminal Investigation Division and Military Intelligence with demands for personal interviews. After those demands were made, the two lawyers were contacted by Magdalena Rosenburg from Rosenburg's Ranch. Both of the men were brought up to speed regarding the actions being brought against the family by the prosecutors at the United Nations Administrative building.

The law firm was in downtown Clovis City, nearby several other law offices. Alfred Rosenburg, III, had purchased a high rise office building, one hundred seventy floors high. The two attorneys shared the entire fiftieth floor. They had three large conference rooms, a computerized law library, thirty-nine offices, eight bathrooms, five showers, ten walk-in closets, two large kitchens and two large executive suites. The executive suites were the location for the offices of Ellis Ragnarsson and Alfred Rosenburg, III. The two men had twelve young lawyers and forty paralegal employees working for them. Most of their business was contract law dealing primarily with the Rosenburg Corporation. They also represented several of the major labor unions in collective bargaining negotiations. Occasionally the firm would go to trial to enforce an agreement.

Ellis had an Executive Suite which was a two thousand square foot office, with a large connecting closet area and a large walk in bathroom complete with a shower and three sinks. Many nights he would stay and work late, generally to have sex with one of the staff members and then he would sleep on his plush couch that would easily convert into a large bed. Ellis had been spending the day downloading the indictments against the Rosenburg family from the criminal court satellite sites. He was distressed that his brothers, Junior and Ivar, and sisters Emma and Ella were also implicated. His father had also been indicted in absentia. In addition, several of the Rosenburg's were indicted. Alfred's father, Magdalena, Carla and other siblings were among the accused.

Ellis was reading over the hundreds of pages of indictments when his law partner announced they had a priority message from Penelope from the space station.

The two men left their Executive Suites and took the call in one of the large conference rooms. After Alfred purchased the high rise building, he installed state of the art security to protect his clients' privacy and for the peace of mind that his family secrets would not be disturbed. The conference rooms and the executive suites were all lined with walls that were soundproof. No one walking by those rooms in the office hallways could hear the conversations that were occurring.

"Computer, route the communication to this Conference Room," Alfred instructed after the sliding doors to the conference room sealed shut. The two men saw Penelope's three dimensional image being broadcast on the center of the large conference room rectangular table.

"Good afternoon, Alfred," Penelope greeted them.

"It is still morning here, dear sister," he responded.

"You look absolutely desirable," Ellis told her.

Penelope ignored the comment from Ellis, "The military is searching the entire Baroness Hotel. They found blood spatters in the hallway and are trying to obtain a computerized match. As you probably already know, they arrested Ella. They stunned her and dragged her away to the Tank. I have the legal papers from a Judge here. Can I send them to you so you can make sure it is all legal?"

"Download them all to us," Alfred instructed her. "We will inspect them. Remain calm, sis. They will demand that you interview with them. Tell them that you will want your lawyer present during the interview. They will accuse you of having something to hide and you will inform them that it is corporate policy. One of our associate lawyers has already been sent up to the space station to advise you. She is a very good lawyer. Just keep your cool and do not panic."

"But Ella....."

"We are working on her case right now," her brother assured her. "Just relax. Before the close of business we will have motions for Discovery and Inspection, Motions to Dismiss and Motions to Suppress filed. We are going to give Collins one hell of a fight."

"Okay," Penelope was nodding. She felt more at ease. "I will wait for the lawyer to arrive. Thank you, Alfred. I hope this all ends well."

Her image disappeared.

"Our families are in for it this time," Ellis said softly. "The indictments look legally sound. If my sister Emma turned on us, she knows everything."

"Everything?" Alfred questioned that statement. "I highly doubt that. My father and uncle keep things from each other. Emma would be lucky to know even twenty percent of the shit our families are involved in." He walked over to a chair and sat down. He unbuttoned the top two buttons of his dress shirt, "I always worried that this day would come. It was only a matter of time before one of our schemes blew up in our faces."

"It is not over yet, my friend," Ellis said firmly. "We have a stellar legal staff and we have bottomless pits of cash. We will find lawyers and judges that can be bribed. Collins might be untouchable, but what about his staff? One thing our two families have proven over the years is that anyone can be gotten to. One way, or another. Collins is widowed; maybe we can entice him with a hot woman to go our way. If that doesn't work I can go kill one of his children and let him know we will kill the rest if he does not cooperate."

"No more killing. Collins is not a man to be messed with. As a Ragnarsson, you should know that." Alfred waived his hand at Ellis as if to dismiss his ideas of more assassinations. "Bribery is the best way. We have a few Judges on the take. Some are members of the Royal Family, just like me. That might be our best avenue for the short term."

"And the long term solution?" Ellis crossed his arms. "The public relations fall out will be disastrous."

"And it could implicate the Glorious Leader!" Alfred slammed his left fist onto the conference table. "My father may be cruel, but Sikorsky is a heartless killer. If this scandal starts to point in his direction he will have his military go out and kill everyone involved and when the dust settles there may be no life left on this purple planet."

"How could Sikorsky get away with wiping out entire cities?" Ellis chuckled at the thought. "The news media would be all over that."

"The news media is nothing!" Alfred yelled at his friend, the stress of the situation was getting to him. "Sikorsky has held power for over two hundred years! You think he will let this go? The news media are a bunch of spineless idiots! They would not know a good news story if it bit them in their collective rears! You are not a Royal, Ellis, so you do not know some of the darkest secrets of our family. Believe me, we do not need this to even have a whisper in the air about the Glorious Leader. When he took over the United Nations, it was not because he said pretty please. He killed his friends. He killed most of the heroes of the wars. He enslaved the Akarzdamedians after he dropped nuclear weapons all over their major cities! He would order you and I killed without a second thought!"

"I did not realize that the Glorious Leader was such a man. The history books characterize him as a man of peace."

"The history books are wrong. They were written

by Sikorsky for Sikorsky and to perpetuate his power by spreading myths and lies!" Alfred stood up and began pacing. "The Calypso was the science ship that had been under the command of Robert Richard Andrews. You do remember that ship from your history classes? The entire Andrews family was on board. His daughter, Judy Andrews, was some type of teen-age genius and an inspiration to all the young people of Earth. Sikorsky had the whole Andrews family killed by firing on them with nuclear missiles. History says that the Andrews family died taking the capital city on the planet now called Sikorsky's Planet. Yes, Ellis. Yes. You see, the Queen of the Akarzdamedians was begging to negotiate a truce. They wanted to surrender to the human invaders. Robert Andrews had the audacity to request that the war end so that the Ambassadors could discuss a peace treaty. Sikorsky went crazy when Andrews made that request. He fired nuclear rockets on the Calypso and eliminated any further talks of peace or surrender."

"I never heard that version of the historical events," Ellis said softly as he watched his law partner cease pacing and stand before a window. "My history classes in school taught us that Sikorsky and Andrews had been best of friends."

"Caine, that little psychotic shit!" Alfred growled. "You remember how we had to cover up another murder he committed a few months ago? I told my father back then that Caine needed to be restrained, watched, controlled and sent to a psychiatric hospital. Father did not heed my advice. Magdalena kept saying that Caine was just 'experimenting' and learning about killing. She made his behavior sound normal. He raped and killed a teacher! Normal? She called Caine normal! His psychosis will bring this family down! I hope now father is in a more logical frame of mind."

"Why don't we do the right thing and just kill Caine?" Ellis suggested. "I know he is your brother, but if we get rid of him then we can concentrate on the issue at hand."

"My father would cut out your heart for even suggesting that," Alfred shot a warning glance back at his partner.

"Fine. We cannot do anything about Caine now," Ellis cleared his throat. "We are both great corporate and business lawyers. Now we get to find out how good we are facing the best in a criminal court. I, for one, am relishing the challenge."

Alfred smiled at that. His law partner had lamented

on many occasions that they had very few cases that ended up in trial. Ellis loved the action of the court room. He was a natural. He had an excellent grasp on the rules of evidence and procedure. Alfred, on the other hand, felt more comfortable pushing contracts.

"Well, then, my friend. You will be in charge of the litigation," he told Ellis as he continued to stare out the windows of the fiftieth floor, enjoying the view of the red-orange sky.

Yuri Gorski and Jen Staszko had spent a few hours of passion and cuddling in his bed. She fell asleep after they had made love for the second time. Gorski showered and checked the news broadcast while his girlfriend rested. His roommate, Drew Harrison, had been introduced to the two women protecting Jen and Elektra. Harrison ended up leaving to their room. Gorski hoped that his friend was able to enjoy the companionship of the new lady and some way, somehow, get over Julia Steiner. The gang had all met at the Academy Cafeteria, less Mejia and the Rhinehard brothers. Even the former members Lincoln, Steiner and Guevara attended. It was a reunion of sorts.

Gorski had taken the words Lund said to him to heart. Gorski knew that he must become tougher to survive as an officer in the Space Command. His hesitation to throw Montrose off the roof would only encourage the enemy. The slogan of the Academy was that "Weakness is Provocative." If Ragnarsson ever escaped, he would not think twice about coming after Gorski because he had displayed weakness. He read the news reports regarding all of the arrests. There was a team of CID investigators and Marines under the command of Major Evart flying over to the Rosenburg Ranch to execute search warrants and arrest warrants. Gorski felt some relief that the arrests were occurring. He wanted justice for Drayton and Elektra.

Gorski felt restless. He looked over to Jen Staszko who was still sound asleep. He decided to take a walk and left his dormitory room as silently as possible. He walked down to the hall to the Andolini brothers' room. He knocked on their door.

Gorski heard a voice beckon him to come in and the door slid open for him. Gorski walked into the room and found Dominic there with Harumi Shigeta. Dominic had recovered from the stun dart poison and seemed his usual vibrant self.

"Hi, Yuri!" Harumi hugged him.

Dominic also hugged Gorski. "My friend. I thought you would still be asleep."

"I can't sleep," Gorski told them. "Where is

Marco?"

Dominic and Shigeta were not certain whether Gorski knew that Marco was involved in a relationship with Mary Lincoln. They looked at each other and shrugged.

"I do not know where he is," Dominic lied. He knew full well that Marco was at Lincoln's dormitory room.

"Can we tell Yuri the news?" Shigeta asked excitedly.

"What news?" Gorski asked.

"Good news my dear friend," Dominic put his arms around Shigeta's waist. "With everything that has happened over the last several days, Harumi and I started talking about our lives, our future and about life and how short it is. We love each other."

Gorski could see that was true, the way Dominic and Harumi looked into each other's eyes. It was as if they were perfect for one another.

"So," she said happily, "Dominic and I are going to get married this weekend."

Gorski smiled and hugged them both. He was deeply happy for his two friends.

Their decision to commit to each other for life came

after a long discussion about their mutual fear of going through life without one another. Harumi was the one to tell Dominic that she was willing to finish her last year at the Academy and join him on whichever ship or planet or space station or asteroid he happened to be assigned to. He in turn knew that he only wanted her as his life partner. He did not have any desire to find another woman. She had become everything to him.

"But when Dominic graduates....." Gorski began.

"Yes, we discussed that problem," Shigeta said. "I will graduate a year later. But, since we will be married, I will be guaranteed assignment with Dominic after I graduate. So, wherever he is, I will soon follow. It is only a year. I just know that I love him so much, that one year will be nothing. We will be together eventually."

"Congratulations my friends," Gorski told them. "Does anyone else know?"

"Only Marco," Dominic answered. "He will be the best man. I was hoping that you, Les and Drew would be in the wedding party."

"I would be honored Dom!" Gorski hugged his friend. It was good to see one of the many relationships work out from the gang. The list of failed relationships seemed endless. Finally one set of lovers had developed a relationship that would be long term.

Gorski thought of Staszko who was also a year behind him. Would she wait like Harumi was willing to do? Gorski doubted Staszko had any designs of a life time with him. Gorski did not want to have that talk with her as he was worried what her response would be. He enjoyed Staszko's company, her sense of humor, her stories about old Earth and the sex was amazing. The discussion of what was ahead for the two of them in the future could wait, but not for much longer.

Harumi and Dominic kissed.

CHAPTER FIVE

Admiral Jordan Seward found the hospital room of young Klaus Rhinehard. The retired Admiral saw that the patient was asleep. Both of his arms were in plaster casts. He had some IV tubes in his arms. Seward sighed. The young lad had been one of the best students, and a talented pilot. He hoped that the injuries were not career ending.

Seward heard some stirring from his left. He noticed that April Mejia was asleep on the visitor's couch in the room. Her hair was messy and her clothing wrinkled. Seward had been told that the woman had refused to leave Rhinehard's side. Seward looked the two over and thought of how much they reminded him of himself and his wife. Young love was a wonderful thing.

He left the room, not wanting to wake the two sleeping cadets. He had a second mission for coming to the hospital. Seward had spent some time interviewing the hospital psychiatric expert, Doctor Mozgov. She was a lovely young woman, brilliant and opinionated. Seward had to make a decision regarding the mental state of cadet pilot Tina Martinson. The cadet had recovered from her coma, which was a positive sign. But, to be a fighter pilot in the Space Command, one must possess nerves of steel. The slightest hesitation could prove deadly. Martinson had lost her composure over the Forbidden Region examination.

Amir al-Nasser died because of her lack of grace under pressure. The Space Command could not afford that kind of loose cannon in the service. Doctor Mozgov had told Seward that, in her opinion, Martinson should not continue as a fighter pilot candidate. Seward, of course, had to be the one to bear the bad news. He knew how much Martinson would be hurt by the decision.

Seward found the young female cadet's hospital room. Martinson was there in her bed, reading a three-dimensional book. The bandages on her head were gone. She still had some bruising and small cuts that were healing. Mozgov had recommended that Seward wait a week or two to have the conversation with Martinson regarding the cadet pilot's future. Seward believed in following the advice of professionals and resolved to wait for Martinson to be released in the next day and then he would take on the task of breaking her dreams of being a pilot to pieces. For now, Seward would simply visit with the sweet girl and see how she was feeling. Although Martinson would never be able to qualify as a pilot, she was certainly capable of obtaining a commission in another branch of service.

Les Gillis enjoyed the hour long walk with Julia Steiner as he escorted her back to her dormitory room. She was always full of some news events that were kept quiet by the state controlled news media. She spoke softly so that others could not hear her, out of her fear that the MI were always listening in for any treasonous statements. She related to Gillis that there were rumors that the lost fleet of Battle Cruisers had been annihilated by a superior alien military force in the western quadrant. When asked where she had learned of such information, Steiner smiled and shrugged, as she always would when delivering such rumors. They had said their good-byes and made mutual promises that they would keep in touch more often.

"Les promise you will keep an open mind about things," Steiner said as they parted.

"What things are you referring to?" Gillis asker her.

Steiner smiled at him, "Just don't be too quick to count out things or people. Second chances are sometimes deserved."

Gillis frowned as Steiner ran for her dormitory building. He was confused by her cryptic statement. Steiner was a blunt person and never communicated with riddles or mysterious comments.

Gillis made the short walk over to the men's dormitory. His shadow, Military Intelligence Corporal Frank Preston, was by his side. Even with the arrests made, Colonel Gorski and lawyer Sean Collins refused to tone down the security. In fact, it had increased dramatically. Gillis could see Marines posted on the roof tops of the many buildings that surrounded the cadet dormitories. Gillis thought that Gorski's father was mobilizing for a war.

He walked into the men's dormitory building and hoped to go by the crowds without meeting any of his friends. As he walked past the Recreation Area, he heard his name called. Gillis stopped and saw Cadet Dino Black pointing at him, yelling his name.

"There's Gillis now!" Cadet Brandon Harcourt yelled.

Gillis watched as about eighty cadets stopped what they were doing and began applauding him. It soon evolved into a standing ovation, a hero's welcome for his actions at the hospital. Gillis, however, felt anything but heroic. All he knew was that two men came to either kill or kidnap him.   And because of that, over thirty people died, including William Bragg. Some of the cadets came and shook his hand, telling him how great he had been. Gillis thanked them politely and kept making his way to the stairs.

Black followed him up the stair case, "Mister Gillis! They secured your room. Your cat was hurt, but he is okay. We all saw on the broadcast feed how you fought that terrorist. Man, everyone is talking about it."

Gillis mumbled a "thank you" to Black and kept moving up the stairs. He was worried about Cosmos the cat. He reached his room, pressed his hand on the security scanner and the computer system opened the door. Gillis turned to Preston.

"I am so tired," Gillis said to him. "Thank you for being there."

"I will be next door," Preston smiled looking past Gillis into his room. "I think you will not be getting any rest soon. Have fun, cadet."

Preston turned and walked away.

Gillis found the statement by the man odd. He turned into his room and saw what Preston had been referring to. Sophia DuBravac was sitting on his bed, wearing a very revealing black lace night gown. Her long brown hair hung over her bare shoulders. Her nightgown was held up by thin spaghetti straps. It was low cut in the front, showing off her ample cleavage from her perfect C cup breasts and her shapely legs were bare. DuBravac was smiling at Gillis, petting Cosmos the cat with her right hand.

"Cat got your tongue?" DuBravac asked Gillis.

She watched as Gillis looked her over. It had felt like an eternity without the man in her life. DuBravac had heard, as all of the cadets had, of Gillis life and death struggle at the hospital. After receiving holo-com calls from Steiner and Freya Cardenas, DuBravac immediately made a determination to give the relationship with Gillis another chance. Her life without Gillis had been miserable. She missed him completely, especially his mind and his humor. She also missed how his hands felt on her body. She had rushed over to his room, hoping to beat him there, and be waiting for him in the most seductive nighty she could find.

Gillis closed the door behind him. DuBravac was even more beautiful than he had remembered her. He had also missed her beyond words. Seeing her in his room, dressed in such a provocative manner, filled him full of the old desire he had for her. She stood as he walked toward her. He wrapped his arms were around her toned body and his lips locked with hers. Cosmos jumped off the bed as Gillis picked DuBravac up in his arms. He laid her on the bed and was kissing her neck and shoulders. She pulled her spaghetti straps down over her shoulders and felt Gillis' hands pull her night gown down, exposing her body. He felt her hand reach down and unzip his cadet uniform. Her hands were running over his muscular chest and abdomen. DuBravac knew from past history that her hands on Gillis' manhood drove him wild. She smiled as she felt him kissing her neck and shoulders. She moaned pleasurably and felt Gillis pull her slinky lingerie the rest of the way off of her. They made love like it was their first time together. When it was over, Gillis cuddled next to her, his arms around her and he fell asleep. DuBravac buried her head in his muscular chest and savored his smell and how his body felt next to hers. She fell asleep, feeling that she had made the best decision of her life by coming to him. Cosmos jumped onto the bed and he cuddled at DuBravac's legs. The cat was purring, as if to tell DuBravac he was happy that she had returned after having been gone for so long.

CHAPTER SIX

Three dozen Raumschiff's were launched from Clovis City and sent to the Rosenburg Ranch. The mission was under the command of Army Captain Rafer Tierney. Each of the Raumschiffs was transporting a platoon of Marines and a few Criminal Investigation Division undercover investigators. The purpose of the mission was to secure evidence regarding the slave trade of the Rosenburg family. They were also to serve arrest warrants on several of the Rosenburg family members. Tierney had the names and pictures of the wanted to every soldier on the mission. The list included Alfred Rosenburg, II, Magdalena Rosenburg, children David, Thomas, Peter, Carla, Juliana and Victoria.

All of the soldiers were in their war class fatigues. Tierney's uniform was all green which was the standard color of the Army uniforms. Tierney had been serving under the command of Colonel Gorski as one of the top officers in the weapons section. They shared history, Tierney and Gorski. They had arrived on New Edinburgh together on the Battle Cruiser U.N.S.C. *Argonaut*. Tierney had been the officer of the day at the weapons control on the Argonaut the day Colonel Gorski's wife had been killed. Although Tierney carried much guilt regarding that incident, Gorski never blamed the Captain for the event. The orders to fire upon that derelict alien space ship came from the Admirals at the Space Command. Tierney had always been fiercely loyal to Gorski given the Colonel not holding the incident against him. The fact that Gorski was a fair supervisor to work for was an added bonus.

Tierney was informed by one of the computer technicians that a communication was coming in for his eyes only. He had the three dimensional image piped into the command section of the Raumschiff that he was in. He waved his hand for the three Private First Class Army technicians that were working nearby to leave.

He waited until he was alone and faced the image of Sean Collins before him. "Captain, I have distressing news."

"What is that?" Tierney asked.

"My lawyers just went before the Judge to argue some motions filed by the lawyers for the Rosenburg's."

Collins informed him. "The lawyers asked that the arrest warrants be quashed pending extradition proceedings to be held in the courts on Rosenburg's Ranch. The Judge granted those motions on each and every Rosenburg that we have a warrant for. The second set of motions was for the purpose of quashing our search warrants on the Ranch. The Judge ruled in our favor on those issues."

"So what is the bottom line, counselor?" Tierney asked.

"Bottom line Captain is that there will be no arrests today. Just search for evidence on the slavery issue and the murders for hire. That is all." Collins' image disappeared.

Damn, Tierney thought to himself, "Computer, broadcast the instructions of Mister Collins to the rest of the Raumschiff's. No arrests today."

Tierney delegated the responsibility for the search at the Rosenburg Ranch Territory to his platoon leaders and the various MI soldiers that were joining the mission. The search for evidence of slaves was exhaustive and went for several days. They found no signs indicating that a human slave trade was being operated out of the territory. They did find slaves from the conquered alien races such as the Saharakaree, Fideerrnekki and Akarzdamedians. The laws passed by the United Nations Security Council on

Sikorsky's Planet, was that conquered aliens had no rights. Ownership of the aliens by humans was permissible as long as the humans obtained the proper United Nations licenses and clearances.

The Saharakaree were four to five foot tall beings that had red orange skin color. Their skin was scaly; their eyes were black and extended from their skulls like antennae. They had four arms with hands that had three elongated fingers. The tips of their fingers had suction cups on the tips. Their tales were about four feet long and were used by the species as a weapon. The tip of each tail was razor sharp and when used, would secrete a paralyzing poison. The normal human that had been cut, even a minor cut, by the tail of a Saharakaree would be unable to move for several days. A full dose of the poison was lethal. The Saharakaree had the ability to leap as high as fifteen feet into the air without a running start. Their major weakness was sensitivity to bright lights and extreme heat. The species was very intelligent. They had been scientists and the Earth Empire conquered their world without provocation. The species was defeated quickly. After their military defeat, the surviving Saharakaree were enslaved by the human invaders. The technology to terra-form a dead planet or moon had been stolen from the Saharakaree.

The Akarzdamedians were cat like beings; most of them were black furred. Some had dark blue or deep purple fur. Their eye colors varied between yellow, blue, green or grey. The Akarzdamedians claimed to have visited Earth over twenty thousand years ago. They claimed to be Gods and were worshiped by many cultures, specifically the ancient Egyptians. The Anubis statues were almost exact in their likeness of the Akarzdamedians. They had claimed the ancient writings of humanity referred to them as "A-I." They claimed that the Bible even mentioned them, giving specific instances to include Joshua and the Jewish army massacring one of their settlements on Earth. Their leader back in that first contact with humanity had been named "Danu" and the river Danube was named after her. The Akarzdamedians returned to Earth in the 2200's and found that they were no longer the object of worship. In their place were Christianity and Islam.

The history books claimed that the Akarzdamedians were livid in that all of their settlements were gone and that they were no longer worshiped. They brought war to Earth. The death toll had been grave but humanity fought back and eventually won. The war had been the most destructive that Earth had ever faced. Millions died. Humanity enslaved the survivors of the Akarzdamedian species and reduced them to slave labor. The aliens were currently used as pilots by some slave traders, keeping control of the aliens by use of computer chip implants in their brains. They were also used to fight to the death in arenas, for sport and gambling.

The Fideerrnekki were indigenous to planet Athena. They were four to eight feet long centipede looking aliens. The Fideerrnekki were able to rapidly learn languages and copy other cultures similar to the way a chameleon would change colors as a defense mechanism. They offered little resistance when Vladimir Sikorsky ordered planet Athena to be invaded and conquered. Many of the surviving creatures were sold as slaves to assist with multi-national translations in business deals.

What Captain Tierney and his team did not know was that there were thousands of human slaves that had been herded hundreds of feet underground to avoid detection. The Rosenburg family had constructed the underground catacombs that led to a large underground city filled with food processors, oxygen regeneration tanks and solar power batteries. They had built the hidden city beneath the surface for precisely this reason, to prevent unwanted eyes from discovering the true nature of the Rosenburg family.

Tierney had been personally greeted by Alfred Rosenburg, II, and was taken to the large mansion of the Rosenburg family. Tierney was in awe of the massive construction. He was truly impressed by what the family had been able to accomplish on the Territory in such a short time period. Tierney followed the seemingly amiable Rosenburg into a massive sized kitchen. In the kitchen were three beautiful young women. All three were wearing tight outfits and low cut tops.

"Captain, these are some of my daughters," Alfred announced. "To my left is Carla, next to her is Juliana and at the other end of the kitchen is Victoria."

"Pleased to make your acquaintance," Tierney told the three lovely ladies.

Each of the women shook his hand. Tierney was under the impression he was going to be manipulated by the women, if he allowed it to happen. All three of the women had been listed in the arrest warrants. Tierney knew their sister, or half-sister, Rebecca, who worked at the United Nations building on Clovis City. These three were just as attractive and seductive as Rebecca.

Carla was wearing a skin tight black and white striped tube top and equally form fitting blue jeans. She was smiling at Tierney, her eyes sparkling in the gas lamp lights of the mansion.

Victoria was the tallest of the three sisters. She was wearing a low cut black dress that accentuated her curves. She was the only one with dark hair and her light blue eyes were alluring. She smiled politely at the Captain.

Juliana was wearing a light blue half shirt that was sleeveless. Tierney noticed that the half shirt she wore was paper thin and left little to the imagination. Her long hair was pulled back by a clip and over her left shoulder. She wore a pair of white shorts that showed off her slender legs. Tierney smiled at her as he found the woman to be the most attractive of the three.

"We wish to cooperate fully, Captain," Carla said, smiling at him.

"I appreciate that," Tierney tried to maintain his professionalism. He had read the affidavits and the legal pleadings. These three women were accused of being in the thick of the human slave trade and their mother, Magdalena, was accused of being a ruthless assassin. Tierney thought that Carla, Juliana and Victoria would be able to seduce any man and kill him easily. They could be the perfect assassins, and here he was, surrounded by them.

"The legal papers claim my daughters are killers and illegal slave traders," Alfred said sadly. "Look at them.

Do they look like cold blooded killers to you?"

"No sir," Tierney agreed with the patriarch of the family. "They most certainly do not look like killers to me." Man-killers or heartbreakers, perhaps, Tierney thought to himself.

"Why would anyone make up such lies against us?" Juliana said with a song in her voice. She was looking the Captain over. She had always found men in uniform handsome.

"We are just normal girls, Captain." Carla told him.

"Where is your mother, Magdalena?' Tierney asked to change the conversation.

"She has been away on business," Alfred responded. "She will voluntarily return to face the false charges against her, just as we will do. Would you like some coffee or wine, Captain?"

"No, thank you," Tierney stood up and motioned toward the door with his right hand. "I must return to my battalion. I want to thank you Mister Rosenburg for the tour of your lovely home and your cooperation. I am told that no evidence of any slave trading has been located so it would seem this is all some horrible mistake. I do apologize for any inconvenience."

Alfred had been watching the Captain closely,

studying his mannerisms and his eyes. Tierney's eyes seemed to settle mostly on Juliana. He decided that she would be the one to get to the Captain.

"Very well, Captain. Juliana, would you mind escorting the Captain out?" Alfred requested.

"Of course, father." Juliana smiled and walked to the Captain and took him by the arm. "I have always thought a man in uniform is very handsome. Follow me, this way."

The trap was sprung, Tierney thought to himself. Their father was very perceptive. Tierney did find Juliana to be the most attractive of the three sisters. His eyes must have betrayed him. He walked with the lovely young woman out of the kitchen. She flirted with the Captain, complimenting him often. She held his arm close to her slender body, intentionally brushing her ample bust against his arm to arouse the Captain.

When Tierney made it to the door Juliana smiled at him, "I hope to see you again soon, Captain. You know where to find me."

"Thank you ma'am," Tierney said politely as he faced her to shake her hand. Juliana leaned into Tierney, wrapped her arms around his neck and kissed him on the cheek, pressing her body against him as she did so.

"Visit me anytime," She whispered in his ear. "I love a man in uniform."

Tierney reluctantly pulled away from the woman as he could feel himself becoming aroused by having her so close to him. He left the mansion and made a conscious effort to avoid looking back. He had to admit to himself, Juliana was a fantastic man magnet. It was all the Army Captain could do to walk away from her as fast as his legs would allow.

Out in the edge of the solar system nearby the eighth planet, a Super-Raumschiff Model XXZ53777 Transport ship was speeding toward the planet of New Edinburgh. The vessel was the length of two football fields and fifty feet high and wide. It was powered by both solar power and a nuclear engine. The ship was fitted with advanced R-5 rockets and dozens of laser batteries that protected the entire circumference of the space craft. The owner of the ship was the infamous Dell Ragnarsson, regarded as one of the deadliest men in the galaxy. He had never bothered giving the ship a name, for he felt that practice was childish. In his mind, a ship was a ship. His crew was meager as he preferred his privacy. He had two pilots, a chef, a nurse, an engineer, nine slave girls for sexual gratification purposes and seven trusted mercenaries that had traveled with him for the past decade. He also had a cargo of three prisoners that were held in the lower deck of the space craft, in cryo-sleep. Ragnarsson had also placed fifty cryo-sleep tubes in a secret compartment with each tube filled with a gestating clone of his oldest son, Dell, Jr. The senior Ragnarsson had been given access to the technology to duplicate life forms by Alfred Rosenburg, II.   Dell had received a message from Magdalena Rosenburg that she needed to meet with him in dead space. She had sent him an encrypted message giving the assassin a specific location for their separate ships to rendezvous. He had been on a mission, which resulted in the successful kidnaping of another human family of five. His orders were to kill the parents and deliver the children. Pursuant to those orders, the father and mother had been ejected out into space and died immediately. The two teen-age daughters and one son were forced into sleep in the cryo-tubes. Alfred had dispatched Dell and his team to bring the three children to him and make sure that they watched their parents die. Dell complied with the orders to the letter. As their parents were forced into the airlock to be ejected into space, the children had sworn all kinds of vengeance after their cries for mercy went unanswered.

Dell Ragnarsson was lifting weights in his small

gymnasium when his computer notified him that the Rosenburg space craft named "Magda" was in range. He set down the dumbbells and used a towel to wipe the sweat from his face. He and Magdalena had worked together for many years as mercenaries and then political assassins. When they began work for the Rosenburg's, Dell and Magdalena agreed that her marriage to the family leader would have many advantages.

First and foremost were the offspring. Magdalena's children would be Rosenburg heirs. They would also be Sikorsky heirs. They would be born into the most powerful and wealthy families in the Eight Solar Systems. The second advantage would be that Magdalena could slowly gain a foothold of control over the Rosenburg activities. The third advantage was that she would stand to inherit a handsome sum of money if and when Alfred Rosenburg, II, passed on.

Magdalena boarded the ship after the two vessels docked. They both walked quietly back to Dell's quarters. He ordered his computer system to seal the doors shut behind them. The one thing they had kept secret was their decades long affair. Magdalena and Dell had been involved since before her marriage to Alfred and the affair continued after the marriage. Unknown to Alfred, some of the children of his union to Magdalena were not of his seed. Magdalena and Dell immediately undressed one another and were on his bed. They had been apart for months and they allowed their lust to take over. Being with Dell was the real reason Magdalena suggested she meet him in person. Alfred was an idiot. She and Dell were able to see each other with impunity on the Rosenburg Ranch and her husband did not suspect a thing. They were able to locate numerous areas where they could sneak off together. No one knew and no one would find out as long as they were careful. She had secretly hoped that her husband would catch her with Dell, so she would have an excuse to kill him. Alfred was a miscreant and always would be.

After they had sex, Magdalena decided it was time to bring Dell up to speed. "Your son, Junior was captured along with Ivar and Emma."

"I know this already," Dell said to her calmly as he ran his fingers through her hair.

"How?"

"My son Ellis contacted me and told me so."

"Of course," Magdalena should have known his lawyer son would keep him updated on all current events.

"He claims Emma turned over states evidence?"

"Yes," Magdalena confirmed as she ran her hands

over his muscular chest and shoulders.

"That is impossible," Dell said thoughtfully. "Emma may have been a bit immature, but she was no coward and certainly not a traitor. Someone else gave the evidence. Ivar could not, he knew little to nothing. Junior would have committed suicide first, as would have Chang and Quintana. Montrose and Nikko were loyal, they would not talk. That leaves that English bastard Prescott and the slave wife, Dulce, as the possible traitors."

"But they are both dead," Magdalena shook her head.

"So the officials claim. I trust none of them, because they might be lying." Dell sat up in the bed, "You know that the militzia lie. The CID lies. They always lie to suck people in and obtain false confessions. They lie to protect informants." He had nothing but contempt for law enforcement. To him, they were all idiots. They could not solve a crime if the solution was hand delivered to them. Over the centuries the evidence of law enforcement incompetence was well known. Jack the Ripper, the numerous drug cartel leaders that never were brought to justice, the Barefoot Bandit who was able to escape capture many times, and the many murders over the thousands of years that went unsolved. And then there were the idiot

Judges and juries.   Clear evidence of guilt would be presented and some Nimrod Doctor that would say anything for a payoff would testify that the lie was the truth, the idiot Judge or jury bought the lie and a murderer goes free. Dell had every reason to believe that his statistical chance of being caught for any given crime was low. There was always someone willing to take money to look the other way.

"So, if those two are alive, who?" She challenged him.

"It would have to be the slave wife. She had no loyalty to the family. And the Rosenburg clan was brutal to her. I almost would not blame her if she had betrayed us. But, she must die, and die in a way that brings her great pain to act as a deterrent to others. It is time for people to learn not to screw with us."

"What do you intend to do?"

"Get my children released and the charges eliminated." He stood and began dressing. "My son should be free by now."

"How would he be free? The Rosenburg's have not acted yet."

"He is free because I trained him. He will either turn some of his guards to help him or he will fight his way to safety." Dell was smiling with pride about his oldest son. "Yes, by now he is free. He will contact me soon. If any of my children are dead, then I will bring death and destruction to those that harmed my offspring."

"Vengeance, my love?"

"No, rather a lesson to not mess with us. I do not believe in revenge. It is an emotional reaction to a loss that almost never results in a positive outcome. I believe that these people should all die as a lesson to the rest of the population. Murder is an instrument of learning. It is a way to instruct others as to the true power in the universe. I will gladly have my remaining resources utilized to teach the people their lesson. The lawyers in Clovis City are all going to die in a very public and painful manner. Goldsmith and Li will die with their families. Collins and I have a few past scores to settle and I will gladly end his life after I gut his children in front of him."

"You still refuse to let go of what happened to Felix?"

Dell glared at Magdalena for bringing up the name, "Collins will die."

Magdalena sighed, "Dell, what did you and your family expect after Darktober? Did you really believe that no one would retaliate? Felix and his hit team killed

Collins' wife. Are you all so naive to think that every once in a while men like Collins might not let it go? Were you really that shocked that Collins was able to track down Felix?"

"Never mention that event to me again," Dell warned her. "I will take care of Collins in due time."

Magdalena waived her hands in the air, "Fine, you don't want to discuss it? Fine!"

"I read the indictments that Ellis sent to me," Dell changed the subject. "I read that there were dozens of cadets and medical staff that interfered with my son. They must all die. I will kill them all personally and have their women raped and their children fed to my pet Dozal's."

Magdalena was growing concerned that both of the men in her life were losing their objectivity. If they were to start randomly killing cadets and medical staff then there would be too much attention brought to bear on them. She watched in silence as Dell dressed. In Magdalena's assessment, the leadership situation was becoming untenable. Perhaps it was time for the Rosenburg children to replace their parents.

Caine Rosenburg had been given the wonderful news via holo-com text from his brother Matthew. Yuri Gorski was alive as were the others that had helped kill

Darryl and injure his friends. Caine ran to the Academy gymnasium and found Avery "Big Bad" Jackson and Cleon Alexander bench pressing in the free weight area. Caine approached them with a big smile on his face.

"What are you smiling about?" Jackson stood up, his seven foot tall body towering over Caine.

"I just received excellent news."

"What news?" Jackson demanded.

"The man that fought you. Yuri Gorski? He is still alive. So are all of his friends."

Jackson contemplated the news and smiled, "Well then, Caine, when do we take a flight back to New Edinburgh to kill them?"

Caine shook his head, "I have a better idea."

"What idea is that?" Alexander was now into the conversation.

"There is a competition coming on the moon of planet Semiramis. The Tournament."

"What does that have to do with us and Gorski?"

"Gorski will be on the team from New Edinburgh. Clovis Academy has a list of names of the final thirty cadets for consideration of the ten cadet team at their Dean's office."

"Thirty names?" Alexander was ready to pound

Caine to dust. "You idiot. That is no guarantee Gorski will be on the team. Plus, how does that even apply to us. None of us will be on the moon of Semiramis at the time of the Tournament. Our grades are horrible and our attendance records are worse. Only the elite cadets get an invitation to compete at that annual Tournament."

"But we will be invited," Caine assured them. "I have paid off the Dean to accept the team that I put together. We will hit Gorski and his team there on that chlorine gas moon and Avery will get to have his revenge on Gorski."

"And if Gorski is not on the team? "Jackson demanded.

"He is," Caine nodded. "I promise you. Gorski, Gillis and Evart will all three be there. The team has already been decided. One of my sister's has connections with the Dean of Clovis Academy and she will see to it that they all three will be there."

"And the referees on the moon? The other two Academy teams? What about them?" Alexander wanted answers. "What about the satellite feed to the rest of the Eight Solar Systems? If we kill those three on that moon, the whole universe will see us do it."

"The referees and the other cadet teams will be

collateral damage," Caine sat down on the bench press machine. "The satellite feed will be cut from the source. I have it all planned out. The question is, are you in?"

"Chin? Lomax? Stapler?" Jackson asked.

"I talked to them already and they are in," Caine informed them. "Are you?"

Jackson thought about the plan. It was plausible. Planet Semiramis was still being Terra-formed and basically barren. The space station orbiting the planet was not yet operational and unoccupied. The moon was also still being terra-formed and there would be no one to help the victims.

Gorski would finally be his.

"I am in," Jackson said.

CHAPTER SEVEN

There were always risks associated with employment aboard a space station. The brave souls that volunteered to serve on a duty station such as that were made aware of the potential dangers before their assignment was made permanent. A space rock or asteroid could, even though the chances were low statistically speaking, smash into the hull of the station and many humans could be swept out into the space vacuum by the explosive rush of oxygen.

Another potential concern that existed was the slight statistical probability that the atomic engines or the solar back up engines would fail simultaneously. The chances of that occurring had been declared a one in a million chance. If it did happen, station would slowly lose its' ability to fight the gravitational pull of the planet or moon below it. There would be a loss of all power and the interior of the space station would be unable to maintain temperatures or provide food. The running water and medical services would be lost and the oxygen reproduction units would shut down without power which would result in suffocation.

Then there was the issue of supplies. All space stations were completely reliant on shuttles to provide food and other substances to sustain it. Some of the newer space stations had become more self-sufficient. They had developed high technology green houses and multi-level food producing decks to feed the occupants.

Space Station CY-7 had been one of the newest models with all of the best and up to date safety measures installed. But the occupants had not been warned of the other type of obvious danger: a sneak attack. So, when Junior Ragnarsson and his three new followers blasted a giant hole into the side of the station, the occupants of the station were caught completely off guard.

Junior had escaped the custody of the Space Command Marines. When he landed on the private Docking Area located on Lynott's Land Territory of planet New Edinburgh, He was able to leave the captured military transport, along with his three new conspirators, and occupy another ship that had been waiting for him in case he ever needed to escape. He had named his private space craft The *Blitzkrieg* after the German term for the style of warfare used to defeat the French in the Second World War. The ship was a converted Super Raumschiff that had been manufactured by the Rosenburg Corporation three years earlier. Junior had the builders install on the vessel the best weaponry available. It had rocket launchers, laser batteries in twenty different sections, cryo-sleep tubes to house fifty individuals, frozen food storage to last years into deep space if need be. The hull of the vessel had been double plated to better withstand a direct attack. There was a weapons storage area with fifty laser rifles, fifty laser pistols, fifty thermal grenade launchers, hundreds of flame darts and stun darts. There were also explosive packs for concussion effect and many others with chlorine and other forms of gas warfare. Junior even had a few tungsten suitcases with nuclear bombs inside, just in case. From this ship, he could fight a small war or even subjugate an entire planet.

Before Junior could leave the Territory, he had to first pay off the Military Intelligence operatives that patrolled the landing strips. Junior and his three new assistants were approached by two female Lieutenants wearing the solid black uniforms of the MI branch. Junior studied the names of the women on their uniforms. The brunette was named Chen and the blonde was named Strossner. Junior had expected them to come for a bribe as that was standard operating procedure for General Tan's Military Intelligence unit. He paid the two lovely ladies five thousand Empire Dollars, in cash, which was the going rate for Tan's unit to look the other way and ask no questions.

When the women took their leave of him, Junior rejoined his three men. His mission was desperate and one that required immediate action.

Junior had gotten word off to his father that he was going to rescue Sister Ella from the Tank on Space Station Cy-7. His father had approved the plan as he believed that it had a high probability of success. Junior had been given reliable information from his brother Ellis, that sister Ella would be in the Cy-7 court room just after three in the morning to enter her plea of not guilty on the indictments against her. Junior sat down with his three rescuers, Chretien, Kulevska and Trevizo, and explained what he expected from them. Thus far, the three AWOL Marines had not committed murder. When they sprung Junior to freedom, they had stunned about a dozen men. Felony acts, to be sure, but not punishable by the death penalty.

Attacking the space station would be a death penalty sanction as there was certain to be many casualties. In addition, the Glorious Leader, Vladimir Sikorsky, often ranted about the duty of loyalty to the Empire. Attacking Space Command soldiers and property was certainly guaranteed to make a person public enemy number one. Junior needed to make certain that the three men had the mettle to kill. He explained to them what his plans were and offered each man one hundred thousand Empire Dollars for their participation. Trevizo made a comment that the offer was four times their annual pay as Marines. One by one, the men affirmed that they were prepared to kill others for the money. Satisfied that the three men were now pure mercenaries, Junior gave them their individual assignments.

He posted his three men on the ship and gave them each specific instructions. Trevizo was to pilot the Super Raumschiff and Chretien was to operate the rocket launchers from the pilot section. The rockets had armor piercing tips that would allow the projectile to penetrate the hull of a ship, or in this case, a space station, before detonating the explosives. The rockets had been perfected over the last two centuries of warfare against alien races that were massacred by the Glorious Leader. Chretien, in his training in the Marines, had learned how to arm, aim and launch the rockets at an intended target. He had also been trained on firing on moving targets. Chretien bragged to the group that his proficiency rating was among the best in his specialized training course.

Kulevska was assigned to operate the laser batteries in the weapons computer section. The laser batteries on the *Blitzkrieg* had been installed by the Rosenburg Corporation military geniuses. Those laser weapons had the capability to pierce armor and obliterate human bodies. Kulevska was also to scan the areas of space around the Space Station and warn of any approaching space craft that might interfere with the rescue operation.

Junior determined that they would attack the space station without warning. In the chaos of the sneak attack, Junior planned on boarding the station and liberating his sister from the Tank. The plan was flawless.

The attack began at just a few minutes past three a.m.

The *Blitzkrieg* flew at docking speed along the west side of the space station. The designers of the space station had built the security wing on the west side. A clear flaw, Junior believed, to an attack similar to what he was planning. The engineers should have provided offensive and defensive weaponry along the entire radius of the station to avoid having their defenses wiped out with just a few well-placed shots. Junior watched from his viewing window as the space station grew larger as the *Blitzkrieg* slowly approached her.   The security operators on the space station monitored the approach of the *Blitzkrieg*, but were lulled into believing the occupants intended to dock. Chretien, on orders from Junior, fired the first volley of rockets at the command station that was located at the top center of Cy-7. Chretien fired the second set of rockets at the weapons defense section on the third floor of the rounded wheel section of the space station before the first volley had even hit their target.

The massive explosion in the command area was devastating. On duty that morning had been a full crew of officers and soldiers, including Space Station Captain Wallace Traxler. Among those assigned for duty that morning were an officer from the Army Corps of Engineering, a security officer, the chief of computers and several other officers. The Captain was enjoying his second cup of coffee and admiring the view of the young female computer technician in her skin tight dress. Traxler had estimated that she was probably in her early twenties. He was thinking to himself that he would love to get her alone in his room. Those thoughts left his mind when the explosions started. The command section erupted in blasts of fire and metal, shaking the entire space station. Men and women perished in the violent explosions. Many others were swept out into space to meet their demise. Traxler had spilled his coffee on his tunic and grabbed onto his chair with both hands as the explosive decompression caused his legs to lift off of the metal floor. He held on with all of his strength as the suction of the space void pulled at him. He watched helplessly as the attractive young computer technician was flung out into space. He turned his head to the right and left in an attempt to survey the damage. He saw that his command station had two gaping holes on the roof due to the explosions.

Traxler struggled to hang on for his life. He felt as if his fingers would break as the vastness of space pulled him. His body was being torn this way and that. Traxler observed as another young woman, an ensign in security, was sucked out into space, screaming in horror. He reached out for her with his right hand to try and catch her. When he did, his left hand could no longer take the strain. He was swept out into space screaming in fear, not wanting to die in such a manner. Captain Wallace Traxler felt the oxygen being torn from his lungs as he was flung past the protective metallic hull of the space station. His last thoughts were that he was planning on retirement next month. He was dead in seconds.

The second volley hit the weapons defenses and erupted inside the side of the station. About twenty-eight Marines and Army service men and women died instantly. Several others tried to hold onto computer panels and metal Doric style columns before the force of the space vacuum sucked them out into the cruel death that awaited them. Chretien, Kulevska and Trevizo could see the metal from the hull of the space station being ripped apart by the explosive decompression, metal flying out into space, followed by bodies and other debris.

Penelope Rosenburg was asleep in her executive suite in the Baroness Hotel when the explosions shook the entire space station. She shot up in her bed and felt another set of explosions and looked around her room with an alarmed expression. She jumped out of bed and ran to her clothes dresser. She hastily threw on a pair of dark blue sweats and tennis shoes. She concluded correctly that the space station was under attack and speculated that it might be an ambush from some alien race that might be intent on invading. She fastened the Velcro snaps on her shoes and ran to her door as another explosion caused the station to shake and tilt. She fell to her right and hit the wall. Using her right arm she forced herself upright and made it to her doorway. She ordered the computer to open the sliding doors to her suite. She saw dozens of guests running down the hallway toward the stairwell, screaming in fear. One couple was clutching their children against the wall, to avoid being trampled on.

Penelope identified herself to the crowd and urged the people to remain calm. She contacted her employees on duty that morning by use of her wrist band holo-com device and urged them to prepare for hysterical customers and to do everything to maintain a sense of calm. After she had instructed her Hotel employees on what to do, she tried to find out what was happening. The noise of the explosions was deafening and she could barely hear her computer responding. Penelope was screaming into her device, demanding that the computer give her an explanation as to where the attack was coming from. Her computer had no answer as of yet, only reporting that they were under attack from an unknown assailant.

Sven Jorgenssen had been asleep in the upper level of his internet cafe "Sven's" in the Mall of Space Station Cy-7 when he was rudely awakened by the explosions and the shaking of his bed. He sat up; thinking perhaps his buzz from some of the illegal substances he took during the day might be playing tricks on him. He rubbed his eyes and yawned just before he felt another explosion and realized then it had not been the drugs.

Jorgenssen jumped out of his bed and threw on his tie died t-shirt and baggy cargo pants. He was walking in circles, looking for his slippers and cursing to himself. He heard screaming outside of his Internet Cafe. He climbed down his antique wooden ladder to the floor level of his store and then ran to the door and looked out his windows. He observed dozens of people running in different directions, screaming. He felt another explosion that sent many in the frenzied crowd sprawling to the metal floor.

Jorgenssen noticed an elderly man near the rails at the mall observation level. The panic stricken crowd pushed the man over the rails.

"Shit!" Jorgenssen said as he flung open his doors. He ran through the crowd, pushing people out of his way. He made it to the rails and saw the old man's hand holding on for dear life. If the man lost his grip he would plummet over one hundred feet to his death. Jorgenssen reached over the rails and took hold of the old man's arm with both of his hands. He grunted and wheezed as he pulled the man up. Jorgenssen felt every muscle in his body straining. He slowly pulled the man up over the safety rails and they fell onto the floor together. Jorgenssen was breathing heavily.

"Thank you, young man!" The older gentleman said as another explosion rocked the space station. "You saved my life."

"Good," Jorgenssen was still gasping for air. "I gotta get back in shape."

Jorgenssen reached into his pants pocket and pulled out a marijuana cigarette and a lighter. His hands were shaking as he put the cigarette in his mouth and lit it. He inhaled and took in a deep drag. Jorgenssen looked over to the old man he had rescued. The old man held out his hand.

"You smoke?" Jorgenssen was surprised. The old man seemed to be more traditional by his clothing and his hair style that was devoid of any colorful highlights.

"I almost fell to my death, young man. I just now added getting stoned to my bucket list."

Jorgenssen smiled and passed the marijuana over to the elderly man. He watched as the man breathed in the smoke from the cigarette.

Junior had already boarded one of his small fighter ships and landed on the Docking area of Space Station Cy-7. He heard newer explosions as Chretien and Kulevska rained rockets and laser blasts onto military command and weapons section targets. By now, Chretien should have blasted the section where the Marines and Army service men and women slept. If he had done so, then the majority of the military presence on the station would be dead, their bodies floating in the space vacuum.

Junior jumped from his ship onto the metal floor of the space station docking area, with a laser pistol in his right hand. He had a web-belt over his shoulders and a thick belt around his waist which was filled with many weapons. He ran as fast as he could toward the prison cell area. He could see hundreds of people fleeing in panic, screaming as more explosions hit the station. He had to push several people aside and even punched one screaming woman in the face when she refused to get out of his way.

After three minutes of running through the panic stricken crowd, Junior made his way into the entrance to the space station Court Room and saw two female Militzia in uniform, a Judge, a prosecutor, a defense lawyer and a few spectators. Also present was his sister, Ella Ragnarsson. She smiled when she recognized her brother. Junior had set his laser pistol on the kill function before landing on the station. He fired two quick shots at the Militzia guards before they had any opportunity to react.

He hit both women in their upper torso. The first died from the baseball sized hole in her chest that the laser beam had blown open. The second Militzia was hit in the lower back and her middle chest area exploded outward, leaving a hole about the size of a basketball. Both of their bodies were thrown violently into the air and then crumpled to the metal floor. The prosecutor attempted to charge at Junior, holding a small laptop computer in the air as a weapon, only to have the top of her head blown off by a laser blast.

The defense attorney, Jada Ying, was from Ellis Ragnarsson's law firm. She had known all along that the rescue attempt was imminent. Ying sat at the defense counsel table with her arms crossed and calmly and watched the action. The Judge tried to run for the Emergency Security Exit. He only made four steps in that direction before Junior split him in half with two laser shots. Several of the spectators had run away in panic. There were two remaining that were huddled together with their arms around each other's shoulders, frozen in fear. Junior shot and killed them without giving the act a second thought.

Jada Ying had located the magnetic openers for Ella's restraints off of one of the dead militzia and released Ella.

"I knew you would come for me," Ella said as she hugged her older brother.

"We must go, before what is left of security gets here," Junior told her and turned his attention to the defense lawyer Jada Ying. "Thank you for the information and the assistance."

"My pleasure."

"I will tell my brother Ellis to give you a big bonus."

"That would be nice," Ying said with a wry smile on her face. "You need to knock me unconscious. Make it look like I tried to stop you."

Junior nodded to Ella. She walked behind her lawyer and delivered a karate style chop to the back. Ying fell, face first, to the floor.

"Let's get out of here," Ella said as she cracked her knuckles.

The brother and sister ran out of the court room. Ella had taken one of the laser pistols from one of the dead Militzia women that had been guarding her. Ella had been instructed in countless hours of training with her father on the proper use of the hand laser. Had Ella been a cadet, or a military service woman, she would have easily qualified as a sharp shooter. She preferred the hand laser for many reasons. First for the accuracy, second the way the laser beam would cauterize the wounds on humans and thus, there would be no bleeding. Blood flowing from a victim was just messy and undignified. Ella liked the fact that the laser would only sever limbs or blow out chunks of the body.

The siblings ran down the hallway quickly. Ella observed the level of panic by the masses on the station. People of all sorts and cultures were screaming in various languages that they were going to die. It was mass hysteria, exactly as Junior had planned on. With the people running about in terror, they would not take the time to notice them as they pushed their way toward the docking bay.

As the assassins continued their dash to safety, Ella saw the fat pig Detective Papalbon directing traffic, calling upon the crowds to remain calm. She remembered that he was one of the CID officers that had been in on her arrest. He was possibly one of the men that had fired at her with their laser pistols. He was there at her bedside after her cyanide pill had been surgically removed from her mouth, taunting her that she was getting the death penalty. Ella recalled that Papalbon had fondled her body when she was medicated and strapped to the surgical table. In her eyes, Papalbon was condescending and a fat pig. He was a typical law enforcement jack ass and she hated them all.

Papalbon saw Ella running towards him and his eyes widened with fear. He tried to draw his laser pistol, but Ella already had hers pointed at him. She aimed and fired three times at the old criminal investigator. Papalbon felt the first two laser beams slice his legs off at his knees. His legs separated from his body. He screamed as his body was falling to the ground. He had his laser pistol in his right hand but the third shot sliced his right arm in half, just below the elbow. The civilians on the station were screaming in horror at the pinpoint accuracy demonstrated by Ella. She ran over to Papalbon and stood over him, laughing. Papalbon's severed right hand fingers were moving still, as if grasping the air.

"Please!" Papalbon pleaded. He was holding his left arm out which his only limb left to him.

Ella fired a sustained shot at Papalbon's neck, directing the laser beam form left to right, and severed his head from his body. She picked his head up by the hair and carried it with her. It would serve as a trophy to remind her of her short imprisonment on Space Station Cy-7. That was one less pig that would mess with her, she thought to herself.

Junior and Ella made it safely to their ship in the

docking bay. They could hear that the random laser fire continued from the *Blitzkrieg* onto the space station. She boarded first and sat in the back as her brother sat in the pilot section. He fired up his engines and took the controls in his hands. He flew the space ship out of the space station without further incident. He looked back at his sister.

"How did they treat you in the Tank?"

"I had to kill one drunken prostitute that would not leave me alone," Ella said as she bounced Papalbon's head in her lap like a toy ball. "Other than that, all is well. I am sure glad to see you. That fat ass Judge refused to accept any bribes."

"And now he is dead," Junior said with pride in his competency with a laser pistol. "Let that be a lesson to all the other Judge's. Take the money or take a laser blast."

He held the half-moon steering column and guided the escape ship toward the Super Raumschiff. "Computer, connect me with the main ship. Chretien, this is Boss Man. We are approaching from your East. We will be docking in about two minutes."

"Roger that, sir," Chretien responded.

"You men did well," Junior complimented them. "You will be receiving a bigger bonus than anticipated."

"Does that mean the mission was a success?" Chretien asked.

"Absolutely," Junior told him.

"Now where do we go?" Chretien wanted to know.

"To kill the damned cadets Gorski, Harrison and Gillis!" Junior growled. "They need to pay for Montrose, Chang and Prescott."

Junior docked the smaller ship with the Blitzkrieg. He and his sister jumped out of the ship after the docking bay bulkheads sealed shut. He was pleased that his three men followed the plan precisely as the Blitzkrieg powered up to full speed and sped away from Space Station Cy-7 at a speed of six thousand kilometers an hour. The pre-arranged plan was to fly away from planet New Edinburgh to throw off the investigators then return to the planet approaching from the opposite side, where the space station would not detect them. The entire maneuver would take about a day and a half to complete. Junior had determined it was absolutely necessary to fly the ship in the opposite direction of their true destination to cover their tracks.

"They are holding Nikko, Quintana, Ivar, Emma and Dulce on New Edinburgh," Junior updated his sister regarding the past events. "Unfortunately, the prosecutor Collins has surrounded himself with loyal staff. The plants in the U.N. building cannot get us good intelligence as to their locations.   But we must find them. If they are prosecuted then the whole organization will potentially be damaged."

"So does this mean that the unwritten rule of keeping our hands off of Collins is removed?"

"I am removing that rule. Collins is a dead man."

Ella agreed. She was tossing Papalbon's head up in the air and catching it. She was ready for action after suffering through the degradation of being arrested and locked in a prison cell.

"Well, brother, I say we kill everyone. Take the whole of Clovis City out. The U.N., the Academy, the private businesses, the private transports and the airfield. Send them all to Hell. We have nukes on board. Let's drop one right in the center of that city and vaporize the lot of them."

Junior shook his index finger at her, "We won't be bombing anyone. We only take out who we need to. Remember what happened to Felix. He always wanted innocents killed on all of his missions. That caught up to him. Remember when we found him dead? I believe that someone that was related to one of his many victims tracked him down. The less damage we do, the better." He hoped that would be the last time he needed to remind her of that imperative. There had been enough killing for one day. Plus if they did such an act as Ella suggested then even the Glorious Leader would not be able to cover their tracks.

"Well, if we won't be using the nukes, then what is your plan?"

"You remember the man named Matthew Rosenburg and his two sisters? The doctors? They showed us those machines. Remember? I took one of them. Or, rather I should say I stole it from the Rosenburg's from their underground caverns. One of the Rosenburg women that worked with Cush and Matthew taught me how the machines work."

Ella set Papalbon's head down on the metal floor of the Raumschiff. "What machine are you referring to? I only saw two that they took from the alien space ship."

Her brother smiled at her, "There were many more, Ella. Some were sent to the Glorious Leader. They clone people, Ella. I took one of the duplication machines for myself. I have it here, on board and I used it."

Ella opened her eyes wide and laughed, "Who did you duplicate? Did it actually work? Are the duplicates on the ship?"

Junior pointed in the direction of the lower level

storage area for the ship. "They are below. Yes I did use it on me. The only problem is that I must have missed a step in the process."

"What do you mean?" She looked over in the direction of where her brother was pointing.

"I have about fifty able bodied humanoids," he motioned for her to follow him. "But each one did not develop properly. Their faces are flat and they did not get my facial attributes at all. The skin color was all wrong. I am quite perplexed by it."

The sister followed him down the steps to a large room that had fifty glass tubes that were seven foot tall and wide enough for a man. Each of the tubes was standing upright and transparent. Ella noticed immediately what her brother had been talking about. Inside the fifty tubes were men that were the same height and build as her brother. But their faces had no extension where their noses were located. Instead there were two small holes which would seemingly be used to breathe through. The location where the mouths should have been had no lips. There was a razor thin slit there which led Ella to question how these duplicates or clones could consume food. Their eyes were completely black. She saw no white or color or pupils. Each of the fifty beings in the tubes had no hair and there no eye brows.

Where the ears should have been located were small holes that would assist the beings to hear. Their arms and legs seemed to be what each normally developed adult male human would have. Their skin color was a tint of light green.

"By the Stars!" Ella said as she walked in front of the duplication tubes. She stopped at a few of them as she inspected the faces. She had the eerie feeling the beings were staring back at her. "Whose brain patterns did you download into them?"

"My own," Her brother responded. "I also implanted memories of certain other abilities that I do not possess. They will do their job in a battle, probably better than I could. They can function just as any man might. In fact, they will fight better than the average man. They will be like my super army."

"So, they can function like any other man? Even sexually?"

He shrugged, "Why? You want to try one or two out?"

"No, stupid. I am just asking. This is amazing. I thought the bragging that I heard from Cush and Matthew was all a load of poggie dung. It really works."

"Yes, but as you can see it did not work perfectly,"

Junior motioned to the faces that never fully formed. "When the idiot Alfred Rosenburg murdered Cush he lost the most intelligent member of his offspring. Matthew is smart, but not like Cush. Not even close. The other Rosenburg scientists had not been able to perfect the process. Thus, you see results like this. Even the skin pigmentation is way off."

"Have you seen Matthew? Is he doing well?" Ella inquired. She had been one of Matthew Rosenburg's lovers for a short time. It had been several months since she had heard from the man.

"I spoke with him a few months ago and he did ask about you. I think you left an impression on the man." He put his arm on his sister's shoulder.

"You realize that father was going to try and duplicate himself and the rest of us. Do you know if he ever succeeded?"

Junior shook his head side to side to indicate that he did not know if their father had been able to create perfect duplicates. Father had bragged that he acquired the technology to do so.

"Come. Let me introduce you to the three men that helped me liberate you. They have proven to be quite dependable and loyal."

"They will help us free Quintana and the others?"

"I believe so. They have proven that they are not afraid to get their hands dirty."

"Where did you leave the Duplication Machine?"

"I left it on my other Super Raumschiff, the *Donner.*"

"So tell me my brother. What else have you been up to while I was stuck on that damned space station with all those boring people?"

CHAPTER EIGHT

Back on the space station, the surviving boring people as Ella referred to them were working diligently to help the wounded and taking steps to repair the damages. Charles Bennington, the chief of the CID, had been interviewing some fact witnesses of a shaken baby case when the attack commenced. He had ordered all of his people to take cover under the large desks. It was standard precaution in any attack to protect themselves from falling metal beams, breaking glass or other random items. When the attack ceased, Bennington beckoned his staff to get back to work.

Bennington sat at his dust and debris covered desk and consulted the space station computer system. "Computer, what happened? I need a damage report!"

The computer was quick to respond, "The space station was attacked by an unknown vessel. The station was hit by twelve different rocket missiles and eighty laser blasts. We have suffered hull breaches at the Command Area, the Weapons sections, security section and the enlisted personnel barracks. Calculating that there are about ninety-seven men and women station in habitants who are dead. Most of the casualties were swept out into space, including Captain Traxler. There are many casualties in the space station as well. Medical personnel are acting now to collect the wounded. All of the three hull breaches have been sealed off by emergency bulk heads."

"What about atmosphere and gravitational controls?" Bennington asked.

"Both are operational."

"The attacking ship?"

"The attacker has fled in a direction leaving the solar system," the Computer stated. "It waited for a small ship to dock before fleeing the scene."

"Another vessel docked with it?" Bennington then felt as if his heart had fallen into his stomach. "Give me the location of Ella Ragnarsson."

"She is no longer on the space station. She was taken to the attacking vessel."

"Damn it!" Bennington kicked a piece of metal that had fallen to the floor in the attack. "Report on the court, any casualties?"

"Judge Santos is dead. The prosecutor and the two Militzia guards are also deceased," the computer told Bennington.

"By the Stars," Bennington whispered. He turned his attention to his investigators. "All right, listen up! There are going to be a ton of scared people out there. Let's go and help out. Drop whatever you are doing. It is time to lend a hand. Come on. That means everybody."

Bennington directed five of his better investigators to assist the emergency room. He took the rest to assist the crowds. They needed to calm down the people. As he left he gave a last set of instructions to the computer.

"Contact Colonel Gorski of U.N. military command on New Edinburgh. Inform him of the situation. We need immediate assistance. Code Red."

Penelope Rosenburg was doing her best to calm down her customers in the hotel lobby. She ordered that the bartender give each of the Baroness guests a free drink on the house. She also was asking the computer for an explanation as to the attack. The computer began to feed her the same answers that Bennington had received. She knew the attack had not been random. There had been no reports of space pirates or alien vessels in the area. She suspected that her family had been involved. She wished that she had been warned by her father or one of her siblings that the space station had been targeted.

Penelope looked out the large observation windows at the entrance of the Baroness Hotel. She gasped when she saw several children wandering around the hallway and many were injured. A few had some minor cuts and bruises. One small girl was holding her left arm and it was bleeding. Another girl, about eight years old, had cuts on her forehead. Penelope bit her bottom lip and closed her eyes for a second as she cursed her father and her family. She decided that she needed to assist the wounded. She ordered three of her housekeeping employees to follow her. She walked outside and approached the children. Many were crying and asking for their parents. She saw the blood coming from some of the wounds on many the children.

"Where are your parents?" Penelope asked them.

The children all were giving different answers. One of the little girls, no more than seven years old, had a cut on her forehead and cheek. She pointed in the direction of the military living quarters and kept saying in Mandarin Chinese that her parents worked up there. Penelope directed her employees to help the injured.

"Children, come with me. I manage the hotel here

and I have plenty of rooms and food for all of you." She repeated the request in Mandarin Chinese, Japanese, Russian, German, Spanish and French. The children all seemed to understand her and she was successful in directing them inside the Hotel. "You will be safe there and I will do everything I can to find your parents."

The girl with the cuts on her forehead and cheek ran to Penelope and hugged her in a manner to show her gratitude. The child released Penelope and walked toward the Hotel Lobby as she had been instructed.

As the children were slowly moving inside the entrance to the Baroness, Penelope saw that Bennington and his men helping injured people. She ran to him.

"Mister Bennington!" She called out to him. "Bring the injured to the Hotel. I have many spare rooms. I am certain the emergency room has none left."

Bennington looked her over. She was wearing her sweats and not dressed in her usual professional clothing. Her long hair was pulled back in a twisty tie. Even though she was not in one of her dressy outfits and had not had the time to put on makeup, she was still a sight to behold. Even her cold demeanor that Bennington had grown accustomed to seemed to be gone. Seeing all those injured children and people seemed to have an effect on her.

"Thank you, ma'am," Bennington said to her. "You heard the lady, get these people into the Baroness. There is safe shelter there."

Bennington looked back at the woman and saw her picking up a scared little boy. He was crying for his parents in the Japanese language. Penelope held the child close and told him in his language that she would help him find them. Bennington was amazed that an Anglo looking Hotel manager would be able to converse in so many other languages so easily. He watched her closely and thought he saw the woman beginning to cry.

"Sometimes, you just never know about people," Bennington said to himself.

"Sir!" Bennington heard someone say to him. He turned and saw Sergeant Major Karam and Technical Sergeant Olivo approaching him.

"Sergeant Major!" Bennington was relieved to see the man. He had always liked Karam and had feared the worse for him due to the attack.

"We are here to help out," Karam reported as he shook Bennington's hand.

"Help the people," Bennington instructed Karam. "Are there any officers left?"

"No sir," Olivo answered. "I checked with the

central computer. All of the officers are dead. Sergeant Major Karam is the highest ranking serviceman left on the station."

Bennington nodded, "I already sent out the distress call to the military on the planet below. Help is on the way, but until it arrives we are on our own. Let's get these people calmed down and to safe areas. I am going to get to the security cameras and download the disc recordings. We need to find out who hit us and why."

"Where do you need us?" Karam asked.

Bennington pointed down, "Olivo, I need you to assess the damage to the Command area and computer systems. Sergeant Major, if you could please check on any survivors in the weapons section and the enlisted quarters."

Penelope was spending her time directing her staff to get the children to rooms. Many of the children told her that they had been in a Day Care while their parents were working. One of the explosions caused a wall to collapse onto the two day care employees. The children, finding themselves without supervision, began walking around the space station, hoping to find their parents. She asked each child for their names and their parents' names. She was going to do all she could to reunite the children with their families. Sadly, she would soon learn that the majority of these children were offspring of the military forces and the many civilian weapons and computer technicians that had just been killed.

At one point, Penelope had a young five year old girl in her lap. She was wiping the blood from the child's face. Penelope had learned from the children that when the wall collapsed at the Day Care center, there were several glass panels that had shattered. She deduced that the broken glass had caused the majority of the cuts on the children. With each child she helped, Penelope felt her anger growing. In her heart, she knew that her family had been somehow responsible for the attack. She looked around her, seeing the children and civilians that had suffered injuries. She remembered the fear on the faces of her customers in the Baroness Hotel. She could hear the cries of the injured, the moans of pain. She could see the fear in the eyes of the children, not knowing where their parents were.

Penelope was hugging the young girl in her lap, consoling her by running her fingers through the child's hair. As she looked on the suffering of the children, Penelope realized that she was weeping. She wiped the tears from her face and thought back to the last time in her life she had been moved to tears. It was when her father murdered her brother Cush. Penelope never forgave her father for his premeditated butchering of her brother. That was the first of many atrocities Penelope had witnessed at the hands of her mentally unstable father. She had seen her father slash open innocent slaves at the Ranch so that he could drink their blood. She had been forced to watch slaves and enemies of the family be eaten by creatures at the Arena. She had been made privy to the barbaric actions of several of her siblings. Penelope knew that if she turned against her father, he would kill her.

But watching the human tragedy before her was too much for Penelope to bear. No doubt that the attack had something to do with her father and the Ragnarsson's. Perhaps to cover up for Caine's sick and twisted murders. All of these innocent children were made orphans in a matter of seconds. The wicked and cruel actions of her family had to end. As she wiped the tears from her cheeks, she came to a life altering decision.

Penelope concluded that her family was out of line and had to be stopped. She determined that she would take every action necessary to bring an end to the Rosenburg reign of terror. She no longer cared about her own life. She would bring her father and her family to justice, one way or another.

"Don't cry pretty lady," the five year old girl in Penelope's arms said softly.

"I am so sorry about this," Penelope said to the child. "I promise that I will do everything I can to help you."

"Thank you, pretty lady," the child reached out with her right hand and caressed Penelope's cheek.

"I am going to help out every one!" Penelope said with conviction as the child looked up at her with hope in her eyes.

Colonel Nikolai Gorski had been sleeping in his home when he received the alert from Space Station Cy-7. His home had an internal computer system that would beep loudly to wake him in the event his attention to a crisis was warranted. He dressed in his uniform and contacted Major Evart to meet him at the United Nations Administrative Building. Gorski lived close to his work and would jog in each morning. He did the same on this day.

Upon arriving at his office, Gorski noted that Rebecca Rosenburg was already at work and acting like she was everyone's best friend. She had been serving as the assistant to Lyss for the past year. Gorski never trusted her as she was always snooping around and asking questions regarding events that she had no clearance to receive information on. Rebecca noticed Gorski walking down the hallway toward her. She smiled at him and wished him a good morning. Gorski returned the nicety and sat down behind his desk.

Without an invitation, Rebecca sauntered into his office. As was normal for her, she was wearing something seductive to attract attention to herself. That morning it was a skin tight red sweater, low cut in the front and a tight black mini skirt with high heeled shoes. Gorski observed that the woman was not wearing a bra, and the form fitting sweater almost left nothing to the imagination. Gorski did his best to try and not notice her in that manner, but she made it very difficult by leaning close to him.

"Colonel, I was wondering if I could ask you a question?" Rebecca asked.

"Certainly," Gorski motioned for her to sit in one of the guest chairs in front of his desk.

She sat down and began, "My father is very concerned about the actions being taken against him. We are a peaceful family, Colonel. We have built several manufacturing plants in our territory so that we could create jobs and make a little profit for ourselves, just like the Allen and Fenster families have done. These allegations make no sense to any of us. Is there anything I can do to show our side?"

Gorski felt the whole premise of the conversation was unethical on her part. The legal team had filed for and received indictments. The legal process must take its' natural course.

"Nothing that I am aware of," Gorski told her. He was pulling out his laptop from his file cabinet to begin the work day. "I do not mean to be rude, but I have an emergency that needs my immediate attention."

"Can I meet you later for lunch or dinner perhaps?"

"No, I do not think so," Gorski was firm with her, looking down at the photograph of his deceased wife, Melita, which was perpetually on his desk top.

She stood up and left his office, clearly not happy that her physique did nothing to stir the Marine Corps Colonel.

After she left his office, Gorski instructed his computer to seal his doors. He then asked for a face to face communication with Captain Tierney.

Gorski knew Tierney would still be asleep on his command Raumschiff that was resting on a landing pad near the family mansion on Rosenburg Ranch. But, he needed to get immediate help to the space station. Gorski saw the sleepy eyed three dimensional view of Tierney appear before him.

"Colonel?" Tierney asked.

"Captain sorry for waking you, but there has been an emergency. An unknown vessel just attacked the space station," Gorski explained quickly.

"What? "Tierney felt the sleep leave him. What Gorski said was more effective than a triple espresso. "Did they catch the culprits? Was it an alien attack?"

"No to your first question and we do not know the identity of the aggressors. But, there was a very high rate of casualties. Almost the entire military service roster on board was lost. All of the officers were killed. I need you, with your background as a weapons expert, to take temporary command of the station. I am ordering you to take your entire company of weapons experts, engineers and computer technicians to begin the repairs of the station."

"But the search warrants for the Rosenburg Ranch..." Tierney protested.

Gorski cut him off, "Your three platoons can leave and go to Cy-7 and not delay the search. There are still several platoons left there on the Ranch to assist the CID on their fact finding mission. Tell Lieutenant Simms that he is in charge of the investigation in your absence. I will request that General Tan send a few platoons from her MI unit to assist us. I need you to get going, that space station is wide open for another attack. All of the defensive weapons sections were annihilated. If you go now you can reach the station in about two hours."

"Yes, Colonel," Tierney acknowledged his orders. "We shall leave immediately."

"Check in with me when you arrive," Gorski instructed. "I will be sending a platoon of construction Marines with supplies to rendezvous with you. I will also be dispatching a group of engineering experts to assist in the rebuilding process. There are plenty of repairs that need immediate attention. Watch your back up there, Captain. These attackers targeted the entire officers' corps on that station. If they come back, they will target you and your platoon leaders. Gorski out."

CHAPTER NINE

Yuri Gorski woke up at four in the morning and rolled over in his bed and kissed Jen Staszko on her forehead. She stirred and stretched.

"What time is it?" She asked as she noticed that the sun was not shining through the windows.

"Four," Gorski told her. "We need to get dressed in uniform for the full formation this morning. Admiral Seward and the Dean are going to address the entire cadet corps today."

Stasko nodded, recalling that the cadets had been ordered to report at the parade field at 0500 on the dot. "I'm hungry."

"Me too," Gorski affirmed. "Let's get down to the cafeteria."

Gorski went to his clothes dresser and pulled out his

one piece, light blue flight suit and stepped into it and zipped it up. He noticed that his friend, Drew Harrison was still asleep with the undercover military intelligence soldier LaShondra Lewis lying next to him. Staszko had thought that Harrison would go for the other woman, Sara Stewart, as she resembled Julia Steiner, but he immediately was attracted to Lewis and her to him. Gorski walked to the bedside and nudged Harrison.

"What?" Harrison whispered.

"Formation in one hour," Gorski reminded him. "Jen and I are going to get a bite to eat. Come with us."

Harrison sat up in his bed and patted Lewis on her shoulder, "Baby, wake up. We have to go."

Lewis was already awake. She opened her eyes and looked up at Harrison. She smiled at him, admiring his bulging muscles and chiseled chin. Lewis had never met a man so physically fit before. She had wanted to find out what Harrison would be like as a lover. Harrison proved to be a smart man, handsome and he was dynamite in bed. She sat up and walked to the bathroom to brush her teeth.

The cadets at the Clovis Academy were all stirring in response to their computerized alarms buzzing. The Dean had sent out a broadcast the night before requiring that everyone be present at 0500 for a formation. The entire student body was required to be present to hear a special announcement regarding the Tournament that would be held at the moon of Planet Semiramis. There was much anticipation and excitement among the cadets. To compete in the annual Tournament was an honor and a great addition to one's resume. Many cadets speculated whether they would be chosen to be on the ten member cadet team.

In the many years that Clovis Academy had been operational, her cadets had never won the Tournament. Several times they had finished in second but in most of the events they ended up in last place. There was a strong feeling of optimism that this year they would bring the trophy home to Clovis City. The Tournament was simplistic in its' rules. Four teams of ten cadets from different Academies would travel to the Moon of Semiramis. For one week, the cadets would practice war games and attempt to capture as many opposing cadets as possible and hold them. When the week was completed, the school with the most captives would generally win. The Judges on the moon could award extra credit points for certain acts. The students would be allowed to take only old style stun guns and stun hand lasers. They would fly to the Moon of Semiramis on a Raumschiff armed with only pulse weapons. The Raumschiff would have four one man fighter ships in the receiving area, also armed only with pulse weapons. The pulsar blasts could cause a disruption on an opponent's ship that would produce temporary engine shut down and ground the vessel. The only other humans on the Moon during the Tournament would be eight retired military service men or women that would act as referees. The entire Tournament would be broadcast over the entire Earth Empire. It had been known to produce high ratings for viewer ship. The United Nations Security Council economic team on Sikorsky's Planet sold advertising slots to the Tournament Broadcast to businesses for top dollar.

The Semiramis Moon Tournament was the first every year among the sanctioned Academies. Each year there would be thirty-two such Tournaments on different moons or small planets so that other Academies would have the opportunity to win the event and take the coveted trophy back to their campus.

The Moon of planet Semiramis was a circumference of 11,112 kilometers. The Space Command scientists had spent the last twenty years attempting to terra-form the Planet Semiramis and her Moon. The process on these two large bodies was slower than other planets or Moons that had been converted into a habitable planet or moon in the past. The Moon orbiting Semiramis had some volcanic activity, but lava was not what was released from the craters during eruptions. That moon produced chlorine gas and in large quantities. The terra-form constructs on the surface were emitting highly concentrated oxygen. But the chlorine gas continued to roll onto the surface. Accordingly, all humans were admonished that, while on the surface of the Moon of Semiramis, to wear their protective enviro-suits, the same as if they would be out on a spacewalk.

Thousands of cadets were gathering in line at the Academy Cafeteria. Several hundred others already had found seats and were eating. All of the graduating seniors were wondering if they stood a chance of being selected to compete in the Tournament. Many cadets were asking, "Will it be me?" Others were speculating on the names of the team members.

Gorski, Staszko, Harrison and Lewis had been met in the hallway at the dormitory by Mark Lund, Gorski's shadow, and they left together to eat. When they arrived at the Cafeteria they stood in line behind several other fellow cadets. The food was served cafeteria style. Each cadet picked up a tray and utensils before obtaining their meal. Gorski noticed that several members of the Gorski Gang were already in the line. He waved at Dirk Fenster who was chatting with Ann Harcourt, Arch Frazier and Elektra

Papanikolaou. Sara Stewart was in line behind the four younger cadets keeping a watchful eye on Elektra. At a corner table, Gorski saw a wonderful sight. Les Gillis and Sophia DuBravac were eating breakfast together, gazing into each other's eyes the way they had in the past. Gorski deduced that the two had put aside their differences and had come to an understanding.

As the line moved quickly, Gorski saw the Andolini brothers, Mary Lincoln and Harumi Shigeta sit down with Gillis and DuBravac. The Italian twins were hugging every one, as was their routine. Jack Harcourt also arrived and got in line behind them.

"What do you think our chances are?" Harrison asked Gorski.

"Of being selected to the Tournament Team?" Gorski clarified the question. "I would say very low. With all the trouble we have caused off campus, the Dean and some of the professors would never select us. We are too unpredictable."

"Maybe unpredictable is what the school needs to actually win for once," Harrison said. "Think about it. You, me, and Les over there. We would be a great core for a team. Dominic is a weapons genius and a marksman. Marco and Mary are fantastic pilots. Michel is a great pilot as well. That is seven. We would just need three others."

"It will never happen," Gorski told him. "Bottom line is that in May, we graduate and go into the draft pool so that the Admirals and Generals will have all of us to choose from to fill their vacancies. Les, once he finishes his Doctorate next year, will get to select his duty station. But the rest of us will be like all the other cadets on Earth, Cootron, Sikorsky's Planet, New Vladivostok, New Berlin, Athena, the Martian Colonies and the other colonial settlements. If any of us here get to serve on the same Battle Cruiser or Fleet, it would be a miracle."

"I know," Harrison sounded depressed. "I just don't want to say good bye to everyone. If we were on the Tournament Team, and we won, we get to select our first duty station. We could stay together as a group."

Everyone was aware that the major reward for winning the tournament was the right to select one's first duty station. All of the other graduating seniors would receive their officer's commission and be drafted to serve wherever the top ranking officers decided.

Gorski had tried not to think of such things and did not want to get sentimental about leaving his friends behind. The biggest loss would be his little brother, Piotr, who would start at the Academy next year. Yuri would be out there, somewhere in the vast cosmos, leaving behind his brother, his father and his lady, Jen behind. He thought of his friends and what it would be like going on to his first duty assignment without them at his side. The idea was painful, yet exciting at the same time. He fully understood Harrison's feelings because he shared them. But receiving their commission as officers was what the process had been about. It was the goal of every cadet to become an officer.

The group filled up their trays with eggs, sausage slices, tomato and cantaloupe wedges, biscuits, Poggie bacon, coffee and juices. A few picked out some pancakes or French toast. Others got orders of chilaquiles or breakfast tacos or burrito's. Gorski also added some oatmeal to his tray. His group made their way to the table with the others.

The Andolini's were on their feet and hugging one and all, including Lewis and Lund, which was a sign they had been fully accepted. Fenster, Frazier, Papanikolaou, Stewart and Ann Harcourt were already at the large table. The biggest topics of discussion were the marriage for Dominic and Shigeta, the reunited relationship of Gillis and DuBravac and the newest couple, Frazier and Papanikolaou.

"Yuri, what are our chances of being selected?"

Marco said before he shoveled a big fork full of French toast in his mouth.

"Marco, we just had this discussion," Gorski said, pointing at Harrison. "Although I believe we would all be great selections, the Dean just does not like us. They will pick from the O'Grady and the Collins group before they choose us."

"But we are the scrappiest group!" DuBravac spoke up. She said "we" which indicated that she was back in their fold. That made Gorski's day. She was always good for Les and him for her. They were a great match. Both of them were brilliant, like walking computer banks of information. And one thing was for certain, Gillis loved her.

Harrison snapped his fingers and pointed his fork in Gorski's direction. "You see! Sophia is right. That was what I was talking about."

"And we agree," Marco added. "We feel that our group should represent the school. We never get chosen for anything around here."

"And we are just as good as anyone else," Lincoln chimed in. "In fact, we are the best. Look at our table. We have the best pilots, the best hand to hand fighters, the best marksmen and," she pointed her fork at Gillis for dramatic effect, "the number one grade point average on campus."

"And he took out a terrorist the other day!" Dominic gave Gillis a high five.

"Mercenary," Gillis corrected his friend.

"And, he is the best lover a woman could ever have," DuBravac said as she leaned over and gave Gillis a long lingering kiss.

"Yuri, they are correct," a voice said from behind. Gorski turned and saw Yesenia Guevara dressed in her cadet uniform, holding a food tray full of scrambled eggs and several juices. "It should be a team from our group. That is, if Dean Harvard ever wants the Trophy. May I sit in that empty space?"

Gorski and the others stood and gave Guevara hugs, welcoming her back to the fold. She sat down with her friends. The group was almost whole again, with only Steiner and Love-Easter missing.

Shigeta immediately sat next to Guevara, "Yesenia, I am so happy you are here. Dominic and I are getting married this weekend. Please, please come."

Guevara hugged Shigeta as she had always looked after Shigeta as if she was her little sister.

"Of course I will be there, Harumi. I would not miss it for the world," Guevara told her. "I am so happy for both of you."

"And, since we are certain more than one of us will be on the team," Frazier announced proudly. "Elektra will have a celebration dinner tonight, with baklava, gyros, dolmas, spanikopita, hummus and Greek salads."

"And a few cases of Mavrodaphne wine that I had imported for all of us to share on a special occasion!" Fenster added.

The table erupted in cheers.

Michel Evart sat down holding a plantana in his right hand. The plantana was a hybrid mix of a banana from Earth and a plorum from New Edinburgh. The plorum was a purple shaped fruit, similar to a mango but a little different flavor. Some of the life sciences doctors spliced the fruits and made trees that grew the plantana, which was absolutely delicious and full of vitamins and minerals.

"So, which of us will be on the Team?" Evart asked. Everyone started laughing at his question. "What is so funny?" They continued to laugh. He saw DuBravac and Yesenia sitting at the table and bowed his head to both of the lovely women. The Frenchman was elated to see the young ladies back with them. He began eating the hybrid fruit.

Evart looked over his shoulder at the rest of the cadets in the massive cafeteria. He was certain there were those that would be angry that Guevara was sitting with the Gorski Gang. Evart saw William Bragg's little brother, Bret, sitting with a group of the rival Bragg gang. Evart noticed that James Cobb was there and he spit on the floor when he realized that Evart looking in his direction. That Cobb hated Evart and the rest of the Gorski Gang was well known. Evart wondered if Cobb liked anyone at all for that matter. Cobb was one of the most anti-social people Evart ever had the displeasure of meeting. Sitting next to Cobb was Roy Starr, Basil Varek, Derek Regehr, Estrellita Calderon, Manuel Calderon, Reynita Calderon, the Lipinski sisters and several other female cadets that Evart did not know. Bragg was staring angrily at Gillis. Evart guessed that Bragg blamed Gillis for the death of his older brother.

"Guys, it's almost 0500," Jack Harcourt told them. He was always the stickler for time.

"Let's go," Gorski said to the group.

They all began picking up their trays and made their way to the recycling machines. With the technology of the day, just about everything could be reused.

As they were leaving, Gorski saw from across the cafeteria that Julia Steiner and Cormac Collins were walking toward the exits. They were arm in arm and laughing together. Behind them was doctoral candidate

Eamon O'Grady, the broad shouldered man that seemed to have all of the favor of the Professors. He was never in trouble and his grades rivaled those of Gillis and Steiner. O'Grady would be selected to be on the Tournament Team, Gorski was certain of that fact and since O'Grady would be chosen, the Professors would surround him with the Collins kid, perhaps Steiner, Blossom Li, Katarina Strahovski and the others in their group. Gorski was hoping that his friends would not have too much of a letdown when the names were read out by the Dean.

Standing behind Cormac and Julia was Gorski's first love, Siobhan Collins. She was walking next to one of her other brothers, Liam. Gorski watched her for just a moment. She looked radiant as always with her curly red hair loose over her shoulders. Her medical cadet uniform was pressed and professional. Her cadet Colonel rank insignia placed perfectly on her shoulder epaulets. Gorski had concerns regarding Jen Staszko and her explosive, violent temper. Siobhan was always calm and collected, almost the polar opposite personality of Staszko.

The parade grounds had been cleaned by the Clovis City technicians of all debris and purple sand residue from the dust storm. The cadets would meet each month for a formation into their specific units and they would be inspected by their instructors. It was on this area that the cadets were taught how to form up into platoons, companies, brigades and battalions. The parade grounds were paved with concrete and were surrounded on the southern portion with large metal and concrete statues of the heroes of history. Many of the statues had been damaged in the dust storm; most of paint had been torn by the coarse sand. Others had pieces of the structures torn loose by the strong winds.

The formation of the over fourteen thousand cadets was perfect. Cadet Brigade Commander Eamon O'Grady was in the front as he directed the traffic. All of his Battalion Commanders behind him and their company commanders behind them. The platoon leaders were lined up twenty paces and centered on their platoons. There was the weapons section battalion, the engineering battalion, the computer technician battalion, the astral navigation battalions, the security battalions, the medical battalion, the scientific battalion, the law school battalion and the miscellaneous battalion which comprised the doctorate students and other subjects. All of the cadets were in their war class uniforms, which were all one piece long-sleeved suits, with zippers in the center from the neck to the mid-drift. Everyone had on the standard issued black boots.

Gorski was in front of his company of cadet pilots. He looked left and right and saw that Lincoln, Marco, Porfirio Cardenas and Evart were in front of their troops. They waited at parade rest for Dean Harvard to present himself. Out of the corner of his eye, Gorski saw April Mejia running as fast as she could to make the formation. She had been spending every second with Klaus Rhinehard at the hospital. Her uniform was wrinkled due to her lack of attention as to her appearance and spending her time at the hospital.

Gorski waited as his cadet executive officer, Blossom Li, called roll for their company. After she finished she approached Gorski, they exchanged salutes and she reported that their entire unit was present and accounted for. Gorski thanked Li and she returned to her post at the rear of the company. Gorski watched as Evart received a similar report from Jack Harcourt. Gorski and the other cadet commanders approached O'Grady, salutes were shared and attendance reports were given. Standing next to O'Grady was his four staff officers, including cadet Colonel Reynita Calderon, the Personnel Commander, who diligently typed into her holographic computer key pad the names of the absent.

Once the reports were shared, Gorski and the other

cadet commanders returned to their positions before their companies. They all waited at parade rest for the professor's to join them.

O'Grady called the cadets to stand at attention when Dean Harvard and Admiral Seward were approaching. They all waited until Harvard and Seward stood in front of O'Grady who saluted the instructors.

"Sirs! All cadets either present or accounted for!" O'Grady said loudly.

Seward returned the salute, "At ease!"

The entire cadet gathering went to parade rest with the Admiral's order. Seward and Harvard nodded at each other.

"Dean Harvard asked me to put together the group of cadets that I thought would be able to win this year's Tournament!" Seward announced loudly. "It was not an easy process. Each and every one of you would have been excellent selections. The rules committee requires that each Academy send only one doctoral candidate and one junior or sophomore. The other eight on the team must be graduating seniors. Those are the rules, ladies and gentlemen."

Seward pulled out his list and cleared his throat. He had originally selected Klaus Rhinehard as his junior undergraduate cadet, but due to his recent injuries, he could not go. Seward pursed his lips and prayed his selections would work well together.

"Commander of the Team is Cadet General Eamon O'Grady!" Seward announced.

"You may applaud!" Dean Harvard said to the cadets.

Many of the cadets began applauding and cheering the selection. Seward motioned for O'Grady to move over and stand next to him.

Gorski looked over to Lincoln and Evart with an "I told you so look". The professors went the old safe way, pick the vanilla cadets and act disappointed when it does not work out. With O'Grady in charge, Gorski speculated that the remaining choices would be cadets that would have been cleared by the team commander. O'Grady would never agree to serving with any of the Gorski Gang.

"As I call the rest of you, please leave the formation and join us in front," Seward requested. "Second in command of the team is Cadet Captain Yuri Gorski."

Applause was heard by Gorski as his name was called. He was stunned. He swallowed hard and did an about face and marched sharply to stand next to O'Grady. Gorski looked back at the crowd of over fourteen thousand cadets cheering. He saw Marco point at him and smile while Lincoln was cheering. Evart was laughing since the joke now seemed to be on Gorski, the one member of the Gang that thought none of them would be selected. Staszko blew Gorski a kiss.

"Third in command and chief pilot is Cadet Captain Porfirio Cardenas!" Seward announced. There was applause from the galleries.

Cardenas followed the example set by Gorski and left his position in the formation. He walked toward O'Grady and Gorski and stood next to the two men. Cardenas did the sign of the cross with his left hand for all to see. He was honored to have been chosen and thanked the Lord for the opportunity. He could not wait to tell his wife, Freya, the great news. He knew she would be very proud of him. He knelt down on the pavement and prayed.

"The rest of the pilots are as follows: Cadet Captain Mary Johnson Lincoln!"

Lincoln was in disbelief as she had been convinced by Gorski that none of them would be chosen. She snapped to attention and walked toward Seward. She fought back the urge to cry as she thought of her father, who was a high ranking officer in the space command. She wished he had been present on this day to hear her name called. She stood proudly next to Cardenas.

"Cadet Captain Marco Andolini!"

There were about one hundred native Italians in the crowd of the cadets and they began singing the old national anthem of their homeland as Marco jumped into the air and began doing cart wheels across the parade ground. That display earned him more applause and cheers. Gorski was laughing as his friend was dancing all the way toward them.   Gorski noticed that Eamon O'Grady was not laughing at all. No sense of humor, Gorski thought. Marco hugged Admiral Seward and Dean Harvard. Harvard even allowed himself to smile, just slightly. Marco then embraced O'Grady, Gorski, and Cardenas and then took Lincoln in his arms, dipped her and gave her a kiss before the large formation. No one cheered louder than Dominic. He was proud and elated for his brother and knew in his heart that Marco deserved to be selected.

O'Grady was disgusted by the display of open affection. Gorski's group showed utter disrespect toward the uniform and the cadet corps, O'Grady thought to himself. He would have made different selections for such an important event for the Academy.

The applause for his performance continued for a few moments longer until Seward cleared his throat.

"Cadet Captain Michel Darcel Evart!"

The cadets continued their applause. Mejia wished that Klaus could have been there, to see all of their friends being selected for this great opportunity. Flora, Michel's younger sister was jumping up and down applauding. Chants of "Viva La France!" were erupting from the crowd as Evart walked calmly to the stage. He shook each of the team member's hands. Marco hugged Evart.

"And Cadet Lieutenant Jurgen Doernitz!"

The applause was deafening. Seward realized by the cheers the majority of the cadets agreed with these selections, it was not mere polite applause. The students wanted desperately to win and felt that these selections were the best. Doernitz walked toward the group, realizing that he was to be the one young underclassman, as a sophomore, allowed on the team. Doernitz felt bad for the other cadet pilots that were juniors and sophomores that were not selected. Blossom Li, Jack Harcourt and many others he believed to be more qualified.

Only Jack Harcourt and James Cobb did not applaud. Jack was bewildered as to why Doernitz was chosen over him or Blossom Li. He looked over to see Doernitz, with a deer in the headlights look on his face, falling out of the formation to join the others in front.

Harcourt was angry but could not understand his feelings. Even though the kid was younger and quiet, he had never done anything bad to anyone. Although he was disappointed, he cursed himself for being inflamed emotionally due to another person's good fortune. He joined in on the accolades and clapped his hands for the fellow cadet.

James Cobb, on the other hand, thought Doernitz was a worthless coward. Cobb's friend, Angus McWilliams, had been kicked out of the Academy and Cobb felt Doernitz rose in popularity due to that incident. Cobb felt he owed it to McWilliams to withhold any applause for Doernitz. Melissa Harcourt clapped for the man that had wanted to become her permanent boyfriend. She had thought of how things ended between them and she deeply regretted the whole break-up. Now that Doernitz had been selected, Melissa was certain many other women would compete with her for his affections. She heard others in the formation express attraction for Doernitz.

Drew Harrison was smiling as the makeup of the team demonstrated that he had been partially correct. The professors finally learned their lesson and, in a desire to win, they selected many of the Gang. The selections of

Gorski, Lincoln, Evart and Marco communicated one thing: that the Administration really wanted that Trophy.

Gorski was in shock that he, Marco, Mary and Michel were all chosen. It must be the end of the world Gorski thought to himself.

"For security, military tactics and weapons, Cadet Colonel Lester Brey Gillis!"

Gillis had been standing in front of the Battalion for the military intelligence cadets. They all erupted into a thunderous applause for their cadet commander. Gillis gave the crowd a thumbs up as he walked over toward the science students. He stopped in front of Cadet Lieutenant Sophia DuBravac and took her in his arms and kissed her.

"We are the scrappy ones," Gillis whispered in her ear. "The things I am going to do to you tonight. I can hardly wait."

"Give me your best shot," DuBravac told him over the cheers and playfully bit his ear.

The science cadets, including their commander, Julia Steiner, were continuing their applause. Steiner was very pleased to see that DuBravac and Gillis were back together. As Gillis then took his place next to the other Team members, Steiner looked back to DuBravac and she was smiling. It had been so long since Steiner saw joy on her face.

"Cadet Captain Drew Harrison!" Seward bellowed.

Harrison left the formation where had been standing in front of his company of security majors. Half way between Seward and the formation Harrison stopped and saluted the entire formation. Harrison could not wait to tell his father, mother and his siblings. He knew they would all be very proud.

The cadets cheered him and he hugged one and all. Harrison bear hugged O'Grady and lifted him off of his feet. "I promise you, we will all make you proud," Harrison whispered in O'Grady's ear.

"You can let go now," O'Grady told Harrison without emotion.

"Just wanted to let you see that we can be friends," Harrison told O'Grady. Harrison did not like the man as he had always believed O'Grady interfered in his relationship with Steiner. He was certain O'Grady was one of the new friends of Steiner whom had advised her to date Collins.

Seward took a deep breath, "And last, but not least. For life sciences and computers, Cadet Colonel Julia Steiner!"

Steiner was not surprised by her selection since all of the previous selections made logical sense. The Dean and the Admiral had selected the best. Her grades were the tops of her division and tied for the best in the entire Academy with Gillis. Her recent showing of nerves of steel at the hospital probably put her name at the top of the list. She smiled at Cormac Collins as she walked toward the other nine that had been chosen. She shook their hands. Marco and Lincoln hugged her. Gillis also gave her a hug. This could work, Steiner thought to herself.

"We can win this," Steiner whispered to Lincoln.

Dean Harvard pointed to the ten cadets, "I present to you your 2532 Tournament Team!"

There was more applause from the cadets. Gorski and the others savored the adulation.

"There will be a celebration tomorrow night!" Seward told the thousands of cadets. "We will be honoring the Team at six p.m. at the soccer field. The cafeteria will cater brisket, salads, steamed carrots, potatoes, beans, fruits and plenty of ale!"

The cadets cheered again.

Seward then told the cadets that the formation was dismissed and that they should all report to class. He turned and faced his team of ten, "You wait; the Dean and I need to have a few words with you."

Dominic Andolini waived to his brother as he

departed the parade field. Shigeta ran to catch up to him and wrapped her left arm around him. He leaned down and kissed her lips.

"Baby, I do not understand. They did not select you," Shigeta said after their kiss. "You deserve to be on that team."

"It actually makes sense," Dominic wrapped his arms around her and pulled her close. "They needed five pilots, a life sciences cadet, a commander and second in command. That only left two slots. Les was the obvious choice for one of the two positions due to his grade points. The last slot probably came down to me, Reynita Calderon and Drew. Reynita is a good cadet and she will be an effective officer someday, but she has never really done anything to set herself apart from the rest. Drew and I have similar grades and talents except that he is in far better shape than I am. Since Marco was already on the team I am sure that the Professors did not want a set of twins going. Drew got the nod."

"They should dump O'Grady and add you!" Shigeta kissed him again.

"I love you," Dominic said and kissed her. "Actually I'm glad I am not going. I get to be with you as opposed to that disgusting moon."

"Well, you are number one on my team," Shigeta ran her hands over his chest and kissed him once more.

Cadet pilots John Gauthier, James Cobb and Roy Starr walked away from the parade grounds together. Gauthier was silent in thought as he walked next to his two friends and listened to them complaining about that fact that neither Seward nor Harvard said any words for William Bragg at the assembly. Gauthier mourned Bragg in his own way, but understood why so many on campus were not mourning the man. Bragg had been unusually cruel to other cadets by hanging them by their underwear on flag poles or forcing their heads into toilets that had not been flushed. Gauthier was one of the few Bragg Gang members that complained about Bragg's actions and had found himself in the minority of the group. He looked back over his shoulder wondering whether he stood a chance to make the team the following year.

The ten tournament cadets had obeyed the order given to them to remain behind.

Jen Staszko ran up to Gorski and kissed him, "I am so very proud of you, Yuri."

"Thank you honey," Gorski said as he held her close. He whispered to her, "I am stunned. Never in a million years would I have seen this coming."

"You deserve this, Yuri. The professors made the right choices. I am going to go to class. See you tonight," Staszko told him. She playfully kissed his nose and ran off to catch up with the other cadets.

After about twenty minutes, the parade ground was virtually empty. In the distance, Gorski looked at the large fifteen foot tall statues of the Glorious Leader and the other heroes of the past wars in which humanity conquered other alien races. All of the stone and metal replicas of those old warriors were facing the front of the parade grounds. Gorski felt that all of the faces on those large carved figures were staring at them.

Seward and Harvard faced their team of ten cadets.

"The selection process was very difficult," Harvard began as he walked back and forth. "There were dozens of other cadets that were just as deserving. But we wanted to put our best team together. What I mean to say is we expect that the ten of you will work together and bring us that trophy."

"The recent incident in the Forbidden Region showed me a lot about the cadet pilots we selected," Seward added. "Cardenas, Andolini, Lincoln and Doernitz, you four acted decisively in defense of another. You kept your heads in a life and death situation which was the clincher that put the four of you on the team. You ten will train, but I recommend that the four of you be the fighter pilots. Evart, you should train to pilot the Raumschiff. Gorski, you are a dual major and can pilot if necessary but your main roll will be to assist O'Grady. Doernitz, your experience in engineering will help out if any repairs are needed.

"O'Grady, your selection as team leader was an easy decision. Your grades, the fact you are almost finished with a Doctorate and your knowledge of military tactics make you the best one to lead the team." Seward paused and looked each cadet in the eye. "I need to ask each of you if you accept this appointment."

"Yes, of course," Cardenas spoke first. "It is a great honor to represent the Academy. I would not miss it for the world."

Gorski nodded, "I am in, Admiral."

"The rest of you?" Seward asked.

"I'm in," Julia Steiner said firmly.

"Me too," Harrison added.

Lincoln and Marco shook their heads in the affirmative. Gillis also nodded.

"Oui," Evart said.

All eyes looked to Doernitz. "Well, um, I am the

youngest one here. I would love to do this, but I was wondering, you know? I was wondering why me?"

"As opposed to who?" Harvard wanted to know.

"Well, Jack Harcourt, Klaus Rhinehard, Pierre Zerbe, Blossom Li or some of the other pilots," Doernitz answered the Dean. The young cadet had watched his fellow classmates and saw the potential in many of them to become great leaders and pilots. "All of them are very talented."

"Because you showed me something young man," Seward spoke up. "I read your file and I know you were taught by Admiral Yamamoto to be a pilot and an engineer well before you even joined this institution. You did not need to attend this Academy to learn the things we have been teaching. You already knew how to fly Fighter Ships, Raumschiffs and Battle Cruisers. You have engaged in aerial and outer space combat against aggressive alien forces. But to be commissioned as an officer, you had to spend four years with us. That's okay, we are glad to have you here. You were chosen because you are the best fighter pilot I have ever seen. Don't let me down."

Doernitz had never told his fellow cadets of his experience in the war over planet New Berlin. He was a young teenager when he served as Admiral Yamamoto's wing man. Yamamoto was a Captain at the time of the famous Piracy Wars. Yamamoto led his Battle Cruiser into battle against an alien race of quadruped reptilians called the Baquello that had allied themselves with some renegade pirates. The Baquello and the pirates had captured a brigade of small Allen Type Fighter ships, killed their rightful pilots and were using the ships to destroy the settlements on New Berlin. The pirates planned on taking the earth-like planet for themselves and had convinced the indigenous Baquello to join them. The Glorious Leader, Vladimir Sikorsky, dispatched the Battle Cruiser *Havana* under the command of Captain Yamamoto to crush the rebellion. He led his Battle Cruiser and eight hundred small Allen Type Fighters into a direct confrontation against the Baquello and the pirates. Yamamoto had Doernitz to fly with him as his wing man. The battle had lasted just under thirty hours and many died. But when the firing ended, Yamamoto had recorded over eighteen kills and Doernitz had shot down thirty-one enemy ships. Doernitz realized that Yamamoto must have told Seward of that battle. "Okay sir. I will do it."

Cardenas put his arm around his brother in law, "Good answer kid."

"Now that is out of the way," Seward pointed to the

gymnasium, "we will be training together every day for the competition. For teamwork building, we will meet at 0500 at the gymnasium every day for weight training, aerobics and martial arts classes. You ten will become so familiar with one another that it will make you sick of each other. We will rotate weight lifting partners, you will spar in the martial arts and hand to hand against some of the best professors we have."

Seward was walking around the group, "Six of you, the pilots plus Gorski who is also a pilot, will be meeting each evening after class at the simulator room. We have downloaded digital images of the Moon of Semiramis. You six will get to know every inch of the terrain and topography of that satellite. O'Grady, Gillis, Steiner, Gorski and Harrison, you will all study in depth the past Tournaments. We have downloaded them all. I want you to see why other teams won and others lost. Keep in mind all of these extra exercises are in addition to your class work. That means no more carousing, no partying heavily. Dean Harvard and I demand complete commitment to this team. Questions?"

"Can I keep my girlfriend?" Gillis asked.

All of the others laughed except for O'Grady.

"Just don't let her get in the way of your training,

son," Seward said after he finished laughing. "Now, we start Monday with the extra training. We have less than two months to get you ready. That means this weekend is your last to go do anything wild. Get it out of your systems."

None of the cadets spoke until O'Grady raised his hand. Seward pointed to him, "I recall that last year's team was mostly graduating seniors. Can we contact any of them for advice? Would that be against any of the rules?"

"Yes, you may contact them. In fact, Lieutenant Junior Grade Frank Glenn is serving on the Battle Cruiser Cortez and keeps in touch with me. I will arrange for him to speak with all of you. Well, get to your classes. Remember, Monday at 0500. No excuses."

The ten cadets dispersed.

CHAPTER TEN

With a heavy box full of files in his hands, Sean Collins walked into his office at five after five in the morning. The boxes were full of items that he had taken as homework. He had accompanied Dulce Ragnarsson to her new living arrangement and, after ensuring her safety, he returned back to Clovis City in a Raumschiff, working on indictments for almost a full day and night without rest.

Collins felt it was his personal responsibility to protect his key witnesses. With the sworn affidavit of Dulce, the power of the Rosenburg family could be challenged in the courts. He believed that the case was strong. He ordered Dulce placed in the polar ice caps of planet New Edinburgh in the secure, underground caverns that the science division had dug a decade earlier. She had a platoon of Marines present to protect her.

Collins set the box if files on his desk and looked around his office. He saw that only a young woman, one of his legal assistants, was present. He was generally the first to arrive and last to leave. He noted that the woman was showing extra enthusiasm and was glad, since he was going to need all the help he could find to prepare for the trials. There would be multiple defendants with several separate conspiracies connecting the majority of them. His job now was to search for all of the corroborating evidence he could locate to support the story given to him by Dulce. In addition to her statement, he had the video recordings of the statements made by the other perpetrators after they had been pumped full of truth serum. The man named Quintana gave up valuable information that Collins considered to be extremely useful in building his case.

Collins understood that a case such as the one against the Rosenburg's could consume a lawyer and take every hour, minute and second he had to spare of each day. But the effort would be worthwhile to rid the planet of the crime family of New Edinburgh.

Collins sat behind his desk and grabbed his empty coffee cup. He needed his fix. He stood up to walk down to the cafeteria and saw that Colonel Nikolai Gorski was standing in his doorway.

"You got a minute?" Gorski asked.

"I have lots of minutes for you Colonel," Collins told him with a smile. "Walk with me to the cafeteria."

The two men began their short journey to the cafeteria. Gorski waited until they were out of sight of Rebecca Rosenburg.

"The space station was attacked this morning," Gorski told the lawyer in a lowered voice. "Almost all of the military presence was wiped out and all of the officers died. The lone attacker was an unmarked Raumschiff. The ship escaped after annihilating all of the defenses and the military forces. In the chaos caused by the sneak attack, Ella Ragnarsson escaped custody."

Collins leaned against the wall in the long hallway with the look of a man defeated. "How the hell? She was supposed to be arraigned this morning and then we were going to transport her down her to the local prison to await her trial date."

They continued walking.

"Yes," Gorski already knew that information. He had planned to have a squad of Military Intelligence soldiers escort the prisoner from the space station to the planet surface. "And whoever rescued her knew that as well. The Judge, your prosecutor and the two Militzia guards were shot dead. Laser blasts."

"Judge Santos?" Collins stopped at the entrance of the cafeteria. "I went to law school with him. He was a good man." He thought of the Judge and the young prosecutor that he had assigned to handle the arraignment. Judge Santos had several wives and many children and Collins knew them all. The prosecutor had just married and was expecting her first child. "I can tell there is more. What else?"

"My Marine squad that was transporting Junior Ragnarsson has disappeared. The entire vessel is off the grid. I think we need to consider the possibility that two of our co-conspirators have been sprung."

"Caging these people is like trying to hold Billy the Kid or Houdini," Collins said at the coffee machines and was pouring a large amount into his empty cup. "You know, with all of the people that are taking bribes on one hand and the others being too afraid to stand up for what is right on the other, we live in a world where we have an illusion of freedom. We do our best to secure safety and justice for the people and all of our efforts are constantly thwarted. And the space station, Nikolai? What are we going to do regarding the loss of military presence there?"

"I had to pull three platoons and send them to the station. Captain Tierney will be in temporary command until the U.N.S.C. sends in a replacement." Gorski found an empty cup at the coffee machine and poured himself some of the java as well. It was going to be a long day. "One of the platoons is from the engineer corps and can assist in the rebuilding of the station."

"We need to bring Secretary General Lyss up to date on these events," Collins swallowed some coffee. "Any luck on the search warrants on the Rosenburg Ranch?"

"None. No slaves. No evidence of slave trading whatsoever other than the legal slave trade of the conquered aliens from some of the wars we have waged. The Arena that the witnesses told us about is there and it does have several deadly creatures underneath. But whether any person had been fed to the animals is not something we can determine. We have nothing and as you alerted us, the courts in the Rosenburg Ranch Territory signed orders quashing our arrest warrants. We cannot even bring the named defendants over here for trial."

Collins sat down at one of the tables in the cafeteria. Gorski sat down across from him. They both saw Rebecca Rosenburg enter the cafeteria. She walked to the self-service line and picked up a tray.

"What do you think about her?" Gorski motioned in Rebecca's direction.

"Other than her dressing like a desperate woman at a night club?" Collins kept drinking his coffee. "Frankly, I have no trust in her. I think she is a spy for her family. She has been trying to date one of my lawyers and I am certain her interest in him is only to get access to our files and information. How about you?"

"I agree that she cannot be trusted. I would love to trap her in some way so we could get rid of her. She is always sneaking around, being nosey."

Collins put his chin on the palm of his left hand, "I could have my attorney give her some fake evidence and we can see where that evidence ends up. We could test her."

"Something we could verify easily, if she were to pass it on?"

"Certainly."

"Do it," Gorski said.

"By the way, did you hear the good news?"

"What good news?"

"My son in law and your son were selected to represent the Academy at the Annual Tournament." Collins finished his coffee and would get another cup in a moment.

Gorski raised his eyebrows in surprise. His son had

so many disciplinary demerits on his file that should have disqualified him from the honor. "Really?"

"Yes, it is a good thing for the cadets. Looks good on their resumes."

"Well, I need to go and congratulate my son in person. I am pleasantly surprised," Gorski said with pride.

The two men watched Rebecca walk past them seductively. She had on a tight black mini-skirt and a white blouse that was practically see through. She was certainly attempting to get their attention. Her tray had a plate of sliced fruit and a cup of coffee.

Collins stood up, "I need more coffee. If there are any new developments, please let me know." He watched as Rebecca walked down the hall. "You know, my first wife had a body like that. I had a lot of fun making babies with her."

"Well, that Rosenburg women has zero maternal instincts," Gorski said. "To her, children would only be a commodity to be used or traded to gain something."

"You are correct, Nikolai. But she would be fun."

"Like dancing with a cage full of hungry lions," Gorski told him.

Rebecca made her way to the office of Secretary General Alexander Lyss and found that he was not there.

She had been ordered by her father to spy on Collins and Colonel Gorski for information regarding the legal case against the family. Lyss, the selected leader of the United Nations on planet New Edinburgh, had been hand selected by the Rosenburg family precisely for moments like this. Rebecca stood at Lyss' door and cursed to herself. Lyss was lazy and constantly arriving late to the office, if he even showed up at all. Rebecca had urged her father many times to replace Lyss, but her warnings had been ignored. She sat behind Lyss' large oak desk and accessed his personal computer that was on the desk top. She read his private e-mails and security briefings. She found no clues as to where the witnesses were being hidden. She sighed. Colonel Gorski and Collins were tight lipped and knew how to keep secrets. She had failed in getting any information from either of those two men and Lyss was no assistance to her. He would wander in around ten a.m. and leave by three in the afternoon after spending the majority of his day with his mistress. Rebecca believed that she could do the job better, but her father would not back her up. She drank her coffee in the dark, scheming how to get rid of the power structure that stood in her way.

Cadet Jurgen Doernitz went from the cadet formation to attend his Advanced Hybrid Nuclear and Solar

Powered Engine Assembly and Repair course at eight a.m. In his class were several of the engineering students and a few of the science majors. Doernitz was the only cadet seeking a pilot major that had registered for the class. Most of the instruction and material had been given to Doernitz over the years that he had been raised by Admiral Yamamoto. But there were some new engineering advances, brought about by the Allen Corporation, that were intriguing. The young man sat down in his seat and waited for the class to begin. The majority of the students were graduating seniors, a few juniors. Doernitz was one of two sophomores.

Sophia DuBravac, a junior who was also in the class walked over and sat down next to Doernitz. He was a bit surprised as the woman had never said one word to Doernitz all semester long. She tapped him on the shoulder.

Doernitz had been reading the technical manual for the class. He sat it down on his desk and looked at DuBravac.

"So, you are going to the Blood Moon," DuBravac said to him.

Doernitz frowned at her question as he had never heard the term before, "Blood Moon?"

"Yes," DuBravac said. "You never heard it called that? That moon cost the lives of an entire crew of scientists fifty-seven years ago. The chlorine gas on the surface was so corrosive that it dissolved their Enviro-Suits. So, they named it the Blood Moon. It is much better now, with the terra-forming machines on the surface mass producing oxygen, the chlorine is not so caustic. Are you excited by your selection?"

"Yes ma'am. I am very surprised they chose me. There were so many others that were worthy of the selection." Doernitz said, although he had never been told of the chlorine gas dangers. He really did not know how to converse with beautiful women. He rambled too much out of nervousness.   "Bull crap!" DuBravac pointed at the technical manual he had been reading. "You are one of the few students that can operate a fast moving ship and, if the ship is grounded, take it apart and put it back together again. I heard about what you did in the Forbidden Region. You do not give yourself enough credit."

"Thank you ma'am," Doernitz looked down at his training manual.

"Stop calling me ma'am. "My name is Sophia." She held out her hand to shake his.

Doernitz reached out to her and shook her hand,

"Pleasure to meet you ma'am...I mean Sophia. I'm sorry, out of habit. My sister always tells me to treat a lady with dignity and respect. I always try to do as she tells me."

"Lady? Moi?" DuBravac laughed. "Thank you for the compliment. Look. I wanted to invite you over to the Women's Dormitory tonight. Greek food is on the menu, fifth floor. My boyfriend will be there. He will be going with you to the Blood Moon and I really want the two of you to get to know each other. And do you see that girl that just walked in to the class?" DuBravac was pointing at a very attractive brunette.

Docrnitz had seen the woman every day during class and had found her to be very appealing. He never had developed the nerve to approach her or talk to her. Doernitz nodded his head, "Yes, I see her."

"Do you like her?" DuBravac asked, knowing the answer already by the look in his eyes.

"She is really pretty," Doernitz said quickly.

"Good. Her name is Lila Zapata. She is a good friend of mine and she likes you, too. She will be there tonight. I think it would be a great idea if the two of you became, friends."

"Just friends?" Doernitz said, almost sounding disappointed.

DuBravac smiled. She was glad the young man could read between the lines. "Friends at first. Remember what your sister taught you. Treat a lady with dignity and respect. If there is going to be more than friendship that will come later. Six o'clock. Be there."

DuBravac stood and walked to her desk. Doernitz could not take his eyes off of Lila Zapata. Yes, Doernitz thought to himself, she was very alluring. Zapata was talking with another student in the class and she must have sensed that she was being stared at. Zapata looked over at Doernitz and gave him a big smile. He smiled back at her. Doernitz decided that he would be at the Greek food celebration.

DuBravac observed the little exchange between Zapata and Doernitz. Excellent, she thought to herself. They do like each other.

DuBravac recalled that the Blood Moon title for the Moon orbiting planet Semiramis had been earned for many disasters. She was surprised Doernitz did not know of the incidents. There was once a shuttle crash on that moon, many years back, caused by the fluctuations in the gravitational pull from planet Semiramis, her sun, the moon and a nearby gas giant planet called planet Tammuz. The shuttle pilots had not been warned that such a dangerous rise and fall of gravitational pull was possible in that solar system. The shuttle smashed into the Blood Moon and eighty-four humans died on that unfortunate mishap.

The "Blood Moon" was a title well deserved, DuBravac thought to herself.

Yuri Gorski was joined by Dominic Andolini, Drew Harrison, Les Gillis and about eighty other cadets at the firing range. The class was Marksmanship 4000, the fourth level of cadet instruction on properly handling, cleaning, maintaining, firing and safety of current weaponry. All senior cadets were required to spend one hour each week practicing with various weapons. Due to the size of the senior class, there were several sections so all of the cadets would have their chance to participate. When they were freshmen, it had been called Marksmanship 1000. In the years at the Academy, the cadets had been schooled and tested on their knowledge of weaponry.

The cadets were to practice with the Allen Corporation new release, the Allen A667 Laser Rifle. The instructor was a retired Army Colonel and he demonstrated to the cadets the proper method of disassembling the weapon. Each cadet had been issued an A667 prior to the class beginning. After observing the instructor, each cadet had to demonstrate they could also take their weapon apart.

Gorski and his friends were able to complete the assigned task with little effort. A few of the other cadets were not as observant and required extra attention from the instructor. They were then ordered to clean the weapons and reassemble them.

Once the entire class had done so, they were marched to the firing range.

Gorski had been one of the better shooters, but Dominic was clearly the best. Had Dominic been born centuries earlier he could have been a gunfighter in the old west. He was accurate and never missed a shot. He was a natural.

The firing range had a five foot tall brick wall that extended for two hundred yards wide. In the distance on the other side of the wall were targets that were three dimensional, computer generated. Generally the targets were of men in menacing poses or wearing mercenary clothing. The computer graphics were so advanced that the targets looked life like.

Gorski and the cadets lined up on the wall and held the laser rifles at the ready, pointing toward their targets. They waited for the instructor to give the order to fire. Once given, each cadet began firing bursts at their assigned target. Gorski pretended in his mind that he was shooting the men that had killed Drayton. He could see their faces and their eyes. Gorski remembered the giant that he had fought on the fifth floor of the Baroness Hotel. Gorski pictured the man's face, his snarl. He fired and hit the computer generated target in the torso. Gorski liked how the new laser rifles felt. They had less kick back than the previous Allen Corporation production and they seemed to be very accurate. He kept firing, thinking that one day he could bring Dray's killers to justice.

In another solar system, at another Academy, Caine Rosenburg and Avery Jackson were taking the exact same class on Marksmanship. They too had been using the Allen Corporation A667 laser rifle and learning the capabilities of the new weapon.

Jackson aimed at his target. In his mind, he pictured Yuri Gorski's face on his three dimensional target. He slowly squeezed the trigger. He fired again and again. Each shot hit the computer generated target. In his mind, Jackson pictured Gorski's chest exploding, or his head being blown off his shoulders. Jackson stopped firing. No, he thought to himself. Gorski will not die with an easy laser blast. Jackson decided that Gorski needed to be skinned alive. Even that was not good enough, Jackson thought. But his death must be slow and painful. Jackson wanted to hear

Gorski beg to die. And when Jackson grew bored with Gorski's pleading for death, he wanted to look Gorski in the eyes as he thrust his knife into his guts. He could hardly wait for that day to arrive.

Caine occasionally looked over to his friend. He could not understand why Jackson had stopped firing. He was day dreaming and certainly not concentrating on the class. Caine shrugged and kept firing. Jackson had some strange mood swings and Caine knew from experience to stay out of the larger man's way when he began acting in such a manner.

CHAPTER ELEVEN

The *Blitzkrieg* had successfully swung around to the opposite side of planet New Edinburgh and entered her atmosphere. Since Space Station Cy-7 had lost all of its ability to scan incoming space ships, Junior Ragnarsson was confident his Raumschiff would arrive on the planet surface undetected. No Space Command Allen Fighter ships had been sent out to intercept them and the long range scans indicated that there were no Battle Cruisers in the solar system. He had monitored the broadcast news reports on his computer system which included some of the news satellites he had hacked into over the years. Junior learned that Colonel Nikolai Gorski assigned three platoons to take over the damaged station and effect repairs. But nothing of the locations of sister Emma, brother Ivar, Nikko, Quintana or his wife, Dulce. Junior wanted to find them all and determine which one had offered evidence against him.

The person that had talked would be dealt with in the Arena.

Junior ordered Chretien, Trevizo and Kulevska to fly the Blitzkrieg to the private landing strip on Clovis City, nearby the cadet Academy. Junior and Ella had mutually agreed that the cadets needed to be taught a serious lesson.

Junior walked to his weapons section and saw his sister, Ella, sharpening some knives. She had six inch bladed knives, twelve inch bladed knives and some other blades. She had a special machine which was solar power operated, that would turn dull blades into razor sharp ones in seconds. Ella pushed each knife into the machine, the blade facing the bottom, and there would be a grinding sound. She pulled each knife out and inspected it. She would continue the process until satisfied that the blade was ready for action.

"Restless, brother?" Ella asked, not looking at him. She had amazing senses. She did not see him walk into the weapons section, but smelled him as he had been walking down the hallway. His bath soap had a distinctive odor.

"Just ready for some payback," he told her and sat down next to her. He began inspecting her knife collection.

Ella had the hilt of a small sword in her hands that she was sharpening. "Payback? Really? Junior, I was thinking that perhaps we could just leave. Coming back here is not the smart play."

"Which is why they will not be ready for us I considered the element of surprise and it is on our side. The cadets think they have won. Let them celebrate and drop their guard. We will eliminate them one at a time. Besides, one of them threw Vinnie over a wall, right in front of me. Murdered him in cold blood. He was my friend, Ella. Hell, he made me Padrino to his twin daughters so I need to make sure that he did not die for nothing. I owe it to Vinnie and to our family name to make those cadets pay."

"You realize if we keep tweaking the noses of everyone, then they will stop at nothing to bring us to justice?" She warned as she looked over the cuts and bruises on her brother's face. She knew that his wounds were due to the time he spent locked out on the roof of that Academy dormitory during the New Edinburgh sand storm. She wondered how much of his attitude was brought about because of the slices on his once handsome face. "We should leave, lay low and come back a year from now to take care of any unfinished business. I already lost my cover and my cushy job over this incident. I frankly feel that father has lost his objectivity and you have, too. They know who we are. After those MI creeps took out Quintana's suicide capsule, and yours my dear brother, they were able to pump you full of their truth liquids and extract all the Intel that they needed. We can no longer kill with impunity. Our cover is shot to hell."

"Examples must be made!" He told her waving his arms around as if to emphasize the statement. "People need to learn to stay out of our way. The sheeple need to be taught to avoid heroism. If we wipe out a good section of cadets, the rest of the humans on other planets will think twice before they involve themselves in something again. Father agrees with me. We will kill about fifty cadets and leave. The message will be received when the news of what we do here gets out. Trust me."

Ella glared at her brother, "I'll do my part and when I am done, Staszko, Elektra and their friends will be dead. I will kill them all for you and for the family pride. You just make sure that you handle your part and get rid of Gorski and his friends once and for all. I am sick of this purple planet and I never want to come back. But when we finish here, they will indict us in absentia and pursue us as if we were public enemy number one. We will have nowhere to hide."

"You can go back and hide on your favorite planet, change your face and identity. Then it will be safe for you. I plan to do the same."

"I miss planet Athena with her beautiful light pink skies, her mountains with the light blue snow caps and the rivers of differing colors. I miss the cool air in my face when standing on top the large skyscraper roof tops. I have hated every second of my time on that metal shell they called a space station. I want to go back to Athena and to spend the next few years living quietly in my penthouse apartment. "

"You miss that pirate boy toy of yours on Athena, what was his name? Alec?"

"Alec. Yes, that is his name. I want to go back and spend time with him."

"Don't worry. By the end of tomorrow night, the whole Academy will be taught a lesson and we will be long gone before they realize the extent of the damage. Besides, dear sister, just the other day you wanted to kill everyone. Now you get your chance and when we are done you can go back to Athena and to your lover."

Six o'clock p.m. could not come soon enough for many of the Gorski Gang. All of the cadets loved the feasts that Elektra Papanikolaou had prepared for them in the past. She had made the events a once a month ritual. Fenster and other members of the gang would spend large sums of money at the local Greek Store and buy up everything Elektra would tell them to. The cafeteria, that employed some cadets as part time kitchen help, would loan the students the large kitchen which included dozens of large ovens, brick ovens, convection ovens, solar powered micro-wave ovens, and dozens of slow cook rotisserie ovens for the event. Elektra would find the day of the month when she would be done with her class lectures before noon and lead a few volunteers to the cafeteria and they would begin work.

Elektra had several students preparing the Greek salad and breaking apart the large amounts of imported feta cheeses. Others were rolling the large leaves and filling them with rice for the dolmas or blending the imported garbanzo beans for the tasty hummus dips. The ovens were cooking various meats and chickens for the large crowd that was expected to attend the feast.

Elektra watched her new love interest, Arch Frazier and his roommate Fenster, taking square cuts of chicken meat and sliding them onto metal skewers for the chicken dish. She kissed Frazier on the cheek. She and Frazier had recently, as Staszko had put it so eloquently, "consummated their friendship." The Greek girl was excited about her relationship with Frazier and hoped they would continue to grow closer to each other.

At Fenster's feet was his black timber wolf, Theodora, watching all of the activity as if she were a sentinel on guard duty. Occasionally Fenster would hand Theodora a piece of cooked chicken and she would chew it with her sharp fangs and swallow it. She would look up at Fenster expectantly, waiting for her next chunk of meat or chicken. The kitchen manager of the cafeteria tolerated Theodora, but it took a small financial bribe by Fenster to earn that acceptance. Theodora was watching everyone with her keen eyes and never left Fenster's side.

The meats were slow cooked and when they were ready, everything was transported over to the women's dormitory in large metal caterer's dishes on large wheeled carts. The whole process generally took four to six hours. The feast would feed over one hundred or so cadets. The invitation list was always tightly controlled, but many of the girls on Elektra's floor were allowed to join in on the festivity. Stasko was helping with the salad preparation as was her shadow, LaShondra Lewis. Sara Stewart was following Elektra around, watching her back. Even though the Ragnarsson's were arrested and the Marines had the

Rosenburg's surrounded, Colonel Gorski had asked the soldiers to remain as body guards, just in case. By three p.m., many others showed up to assist, among them Lila Zapata, Sophia DuBravac, Melissa Harcourt, Flora Evart, Supreet Patel, Drew Harrison and Yuri Gorski's little brother, Piotr.

At six p.m., the cadets were pushing the carts of the prepared food across the paved walkways toward the women's dormitory. Lewis and Stewart were watching their assignments closely, as they had been informed that the two Ragnarsson siblings escaped custody. The two operatives feared that it was only a matter of time before the assassins would learn that their sister, Emma, was dead and their brother Ivar had been tortured by Staszko. They would come for revenge, sooner or later.

The women's dormitory was full of celebration as the food was being passed out on plates to the invited guests. Fenster, Ann Harcourt and Supreet Patel were opening bottles of imported Greek wine and pouring the dark red drink into glasses quickly. The demand was huge and the three worked hard to keep up with the outstretched hands of guests. Theodora sat at Fenster's feet, sniffing each person that approached them.

The crowd cheered when Klaus Rhinehard and

April Mejia entered the hallway. Everyone had hoped that Klaus would be released from the hospital that day. He raised his arms up to show off his two plastic wrapped arms. Behind him was his brother, Rolf. The crowd moved against the walls so that the three cadets could get to the front of the food line. Elektra, Stewart, Staszko, Lewis and Melissa Harcourt were the servers and prepared plates for them. They all welcomed him with hugs and Klaus was thankful to one and all. Mejia took his plate for him and took him back to her room that she shared with Harumi Shigeta.

Yuri Gorski arrived and was shaking hands when he saw his little brother talking to Cadet Mia Nguyen.

Yuri gave his brother a hug, "Glad you made it!"

"Thanks for the invite, Yuri," Piotr Gorski said. He admired, even worshiped his big brother. Piotr was six years younger, only sixteen, but his big brother was able to sneak him into events that most sixteen year olds were never able to experience. He wanted to grow up to be just like Yuri. "And, congratulations on being selected to the team. Dad is going to be really proud of you."

"I think dad is going to be as stunned as I was. This is a great week. We get selected to the tournament, Harumi and Dominic are getting married and we celebrate a bonfire tomorrow night. Life is great."

Some glasses of wine made down to the Gorski brothers. They took the glasses and clinked them together. "Na Zdorovie," the two brothers said in unison and took a sip.   Yuri and Piotr had always been close, but Piotr did not share his older brothers' mistrust of authority. Piotr believed in law and order, good and evil, and that humanity was inherently beneficent and moral. Whereas Yuri, due to his viewing the death of their mother at the hands of Space Command officers, believed that good and evil came in different forms and rarely where one would expect it. Yuri questioned authority regularly, while Piotr accepted all he was told or instructed.

"That is really good!" Piotr said. "Ah, my manners, Yuri do you know Mia Nguyen?"

"Yes, of course," he shook the young woman's hand. Nguyen was seventeen, a freshman, from a family of Vietnamese descendants on New Edinburgh. Her family owned and operated a few profitable restaurants on Clovis City and Lynott's Land. She was about three inches over five feet tall, with long dark hair and slender build. It was no secret that Piotr found Nguyen attractive. Every time Piotr and Yuri would talk, the little Gorski would ask the older if he had seen Nguyen that day.

"Good to see you," Nguyen told Yuri.

"You two have fun!" Yuri said, not wanting to harm Piotr's chances with the lady by dominating the conversation. "I have to find my girl."

Yuri left the couple and walked through the crowd, found the food line and walked behind the rows of trays to Jen Staszko. He put his arms around her toned waist and kissed her on the lips. "I missed you all day long."

"Me too," Staszko smiled. She loved it when he would take charge, grab her and pull her to him. "Would I be able to interest you in a Greek Salad with feta cheese, olives, tomato wedges, red onion slices and...."

Gorski kissed her on the lips again, "Serve me up babe. It is time for a celebration."

Mark Lund, Gorski's shadow, was in the background, watching everyone. He was given a large plate of food, which he readily accepted. He was starving. He politely refused the offer of wine and chose a bottle of water to drink instead. Lund was worried that the escaped Ragnarsson's would return to claim vengeance for their fallen comrades. The Ragnarsson's were smart, well trained and sneaky. They would come and attack when one was least prepared for it. Lund wanted to be sharp and on his toes at all times. An attractive female cadet in tube top and tight shorts began making small talk with Lund in an effort to get to know him. He and his fellow operatives were still operating under the fiction that they were cadets at the Academy. Lund found the woman to have a pleasant personality and he politely conversed with her as he kept his eyes on Yuri Gorski.

Michel Evart arrived a bit later than the other cadets with his new shadow following behind him. His name was Benjamen Zhao, a staff sergeant and a well-trained member of the Military Intelligence branch. Zhao had blended in well with the cadets as he had a baby face and looked young. Underneath his baggy shirt, Zhao had two laser pistols ready. He was ambidextrous and able to fire with both hands at the same time with effective results. Zhao had been born and raised on Sikorsky's Planet. His parents had been seventh generation citizens of his home planet. At the age of seventeen, he enlisted to serve in the Space Command. Planet New Edinburgh had been his third assignment. Zhao ate his plate down the hall from Evart, but watched him out of the corner of his eyes.

Les Gillis had gone back to his dormitory room after class to check on Cosmos the cat and had spent some time playing with him, using a cat toy on a string. Gillis' shadow, Frank Preston, sat on Love-Easter's old bed, checking his knives for their sharpness, laser pistols for their energy levels and silently counted his stun dart inventory. He was extra vigilant, after being informed that the Ragnarsson's had escaped custody. Gillis finally decided it was time to eat and went to the other dormitory to join the party. Preston followed him, watching above and behind them constantly.

Gillis had grown to like Preston. He had demonstrated from his actions that he was a good man, loyal and interesting to speak with. Gillis had learned that Preston had served as a guard before on the Martian colonies. Preston did not tell Gillis that he had failed in that previous assignment. The man Preston had been guarding on Mars was killed in an explosion and Preston had sworn to himself he would not fail again. He had grown to respect Gillis and would jump on a thermite grenade for him if need be.

As they walked into the hallway of the celebration, Preston watched as DuBravac jumped into Gillis arms, kissing him passionately with her legs locked around his mid-section. Gillis had his arms around her, holding her tight and kissed her back. He loved how affectionate she was. DuBravac slowly slid down Gillis body and turned his attention to the opposite wall. Gillis saw one of

DuBravac's engineering friends standing there, watching them with wide eyes.

"Honey, this is my friend, Lila Zapata."

Gillis extended his hand to her, "I have seen you around. Pleasure to finally meet you."

"Pleased to meet you," Zapata told him and then turned her head to DuBravac. "Are you guys allowed to do stuff like that in public?"

"Come on Lila," DuBravac laughed. "Everywhere we go we see holographic pictures and three dimensional broadcasts from The Glorious Leader, urging us to breed and make babies. Nudity is everywhere. You see it all over. Plus, we all have to start taking those fertility drugs at age seventeen. Those things dramatically increase the sex drive and sperm and egg counts. The government doesn't just expect us to have sex, it demands it."

Zapata nodded, "So, am I breaking any laws by not having a boyfriend?"

DuBravac took her by the arm, "Lila, you are so silly. It isn't your fault that your last date got burned to death the other night. Relax. I can feel how tense you are."

Zapata looked down at her feet, recalling her part in the dormitory attack. She and her date had charged out onto the rooftop of the dormitory during the sand storm in an effort to help Yuri Gorski and his friends. Her date, an engineering cadet named LeJeferiez, had been struck by one of the flame darts and he was roasted alive. Zapata had only dated the man once, but she had really liked him. She still felt bad about the death and the way he had died was horrifying. He had wanted to help Gorski and Harrison, as had she. It was a night she would not forget.

"I will relax Sophia. I promise. It's just that Jurgen is so dreamy."

"Dreamy?" DuBravac looked at Zapata. "I never heard such a term before. Look, I screened Doernitz. That boy likes you a lot. And what man would not. You have the most fantastic ass of all the women in the Academy. He is already yours and you just don't realize it."

Zapata swallowed, and followed her friend. She had been told by other men that she was "bootylicious," and that she was "a hot tamale" and she had been propositioned for sex many times. At many gatherings men would grab her butt without permission, making excuses that she was so fine that they were compelled to grab her. She had been born on the Earth's moon and raised in many different space ships as her mother and father served the Space Command. When she turned seventeen, she left her family to follow in their footsteps and study to become an officer.

Her parents had raised her to ignore the government sponsored propaganda to have sex with any man that wanted her. They taught her to find one man to love, marry and have a family with. Based on her background, the boldness in which men and women acted at the Academy was difficult for her to accept.

Zapata took to heart the advice of her parents, no sleeping around until she knew she was in a long term relationship.

Zapata noticed Doernitz in the food line with Marco and Lincoln. Marco had taken a liking to Doernitz and was introducing him to many of the other cadets. As they were accepting their plates of food when Doernitz turned and noticed Gillis, DuBravac, Zapata and Preston approaching.

DuBravac had been the mover and shaker of the group. Some had called her a social butterfly others called her the party coordinator. She immediately walked ahead of everyone and hugged Lincoln and Marco. She whispered into Lincoln's ear, "I need to borrow Jurgen. I think he and Lila should become friends."

Lincoln moved her eyes from Zapata to Doernitz and observed how the two younger cadets were looking at one another.

"Friends, huh? Looks to me there may be much

more than friendship in the minds of those two."

"That's what I am hoping for," DuBravac smiled then she turned to collect Doernitz but noticed he already had walked to Zapata. DuBravac stroked her chin with her fingers and watched as Doernitz gave Zapata a fresh plate of food and a glass of wine. "I'll be damned."

Doernitz had decided to be bold and took the lovely lady a fresh plate of food and wine to wash it down with. He had asked his sister and her husband how to properly introduce himself to the lady. They both had instructed him to take her something, wine, food and offer the items to her and simply say: "Hi, I am Jurgen."

Zapata took the plate of food in her left hand and the wine in her right, "I'm Lila."

"I know," Doernitz said. "I was told you and I should become friends."

Zapata drank a gulp of the wine, nervous about saying the right thing to the young man. Her constant studying and learning caused her to not socialize much. She wanted to get to know Doernitz, but was unsure of herself.

"Me too. I mean, I was told the same thing about you."

"Let's go somewhere we can talk," Doernitz suggested. He had never been so close to her before. He saw her light brown eyes, her smile, and the dimples in her cheeks. She was a beautiful woman.

"My room is down the hall," Zapata suggested as she was impressed by the good looks of the young man before her.

"Lead the way."

Lincoln, who had been watching the interaction between the two shy cadets, laughed and turned to face DuBravac, "Looks like those two figured it all out on their own."

Gillis had caught up to DuBravac and noticed that she was speaking with Lincoln. He hugged her and whispered into her ear, "Anything exciting I should know about?"

"No," DuBravac answered him as she watched Zapata lead Doernitz to her dormitory room. "All is well."

Unknown to DuBravac, Lincoln, Gillis or Marco, Melissa Harcourt had been watching Doernitz at the other end of the hallway. The Child of Athena was grinding her teeth in anger. Doernitz had been hers. Even though she had cast him aside, Melissa had decided she was not yet finished with him. She planned on ensuring no further interference from little Zapata.

CHAPTER TWELVE

Preparing to kill had become fairly routine for Ella Ragnarsson. She had lost count of the number of victims she terminated over the years. She paid attention to every detail, especially concealing her appearance, so that she could avoid any witnesses identifying her. She was dressed in a one piece solid black suit and had a web belt around her waist and shoulders that contained a dozen newly sharpened knives, two laser pistols, stun darts, flame darts, and light intensifying goggles. She had also tied a black cloak around her neck and pulled its' hood over her head. The special cloak had been created a few years back by scientists from the Breckenridge Corporation. For years the scientists searched for a method to make a person 'invisible' to the human eye. Ella had used the cloaks of concealment in the past to take out a target. The cloak went from head to toe and created the illusion of invisibility and her targets would be unable to see her coming. The best they might see would be her shadow, but nothing more. The cloaks had been outlawed by the Space Command, but the Ragnarsson family had stolen dozens from the Breckenridge family factories on Earth and regularly used them in assassination attempts.

Ella also had a few dozen razor thin plastic leg and arm binders to tie up her hostages. The last item she added to her arsenal was a small plastic cup with a screw top which contained one hundred pills of Red Dust. She knew that the enemy was going to celebrate a big event in the evening. She planned on using the drugs to neutralize the majority of the student body by poisoning the water supply. The Red Dust would cause the ones that ingested the substance to hallucinate and not react as normal. Once the drug took effect, the cadet targets would all be easy to kill or eliminate. Ella put on a pair of black boots that were made with the same substance as the cloak so that her feet would not be detected. She began burning a cork from a wine bottle with a cigarette lighter. After she burned the cork she used it to make black streaks on her cheeks, forehead and chin until she had broken up the contours of her face. She looked in a mirror and smiled; satisfied that she was prepared to begin her mission.

Junior had given specific instructions to Trevizo,

Chretien and Kulevska to set up a perimeter around the Clovis City Rattlesnakes soccer field. There was one man on the south, one on the east and one on the west. They would be responsible for firing stun blasts into the crowds and forcing them to the north entrance, where Junior would be waiting to take out his targets. He had coordinated with his sister how the attack would proceed. She would sneak onto the field through use of stealth, and begin to eliminate the female targets.

Once the bodies started to pile up, confusion would reign and panic would begin. The crowd would attempt to flee and quickly find that three of the four exits were covered, forcing Gorski and his friends to the north entrance. Junior held one of the large knives his sister had sharpened and looked forward to thrusting the blade into Gorski.

Junior had his weaponry prepared and the faces of those that needed to die memorized. He hoped to take a few prisoners, for some leisurely torturing and fileting. The animals at the Arena needed to be fed some fresh human meat as well. He checked his hand lasers and they were fully charged. He enjoyed the hunt, but his favorite past time was to attend the funerals of those he had killed. Watching the mourners and hear their cries of anguish brought him satisfaction. He had learned the pleasure of attending funerals of the targets from his father. When the wails of despair and the crying started, Junior felt as if he had accomplished something wonderful. He brought the world of the deceased family to an end. Their lives would be changed forever thanks to the loss of the loved one and he was the one to receive the joy for causing the grief of others. He believed that he made a difference in the lives of others each time he killed.

The sun over New Edinburgh had set and it was now pitch black outside. The party at the women's dormitory was a rousing success as many cadets were drunk on wine; others had stuffed themselves with gyros or other tasty dishes. Staszko and Gorski helped Papanikolaou, Frazier, Fenster, Flora and Patel pick up the dishes so that they could be carted back to the cafeteria for cleaning. Earlier, the Andolini twins left the gathering with Mary and Harumi.

Harrison had stayed behind to spend more time with Lewis. As she was talking to Harrison Lewis kept her eyes on Staszko. Stewart was also vigilant as she made small talk with a female cadet named Farinelli.

Gorski noted that Lund had been spending some time speaking with some of the other cadets, giving Gorski privacy to spend time with his friends. But Lund was always there hanging in the background and ready for action. Gorski noticed that Lund was deep in conversation with one of the widows of Amir al-Nasser. Gorski recalled that the woman's name was Nazeen. She had long curly dark hair and lovely eyes. Lund spent the entire evening conversing with her.

Gorski and Staszko eventually said their good-byes and left the party and Lund politely said good night to Nazeen al-Nasser to free himself and follow Gorski.

Gillis and DuBravac were the last two hold overs and walked to her dormitory room with Frank Preston lurking behind them. Gillis held DuBravac in his arms and kissed her passionately. He enjoyed the way her body felt next to him.

"So, are you going to open the door?" Gillis asked between kisses.

"Computer, open the door," DuBravac instructed.

The doors slid open and Gillis and DuBravac were kissing wildly as they stepped into the room. Gillis was unzipping the front of DuBravac's uniform when they both heard someone clear their throat. The two stopped kissing and saw that Doernitz sitting on the floor with Zapata, playing computer generated three dimensional chess, in which the chess board was glowing gold and black for the space squares and the chess pieces were the traditional black and white color, Vikings versus Romans.

"Sorry," Zapata said, embarrassed. She was lying on her stomach, her elbows on the floor and her palms of her hands cradling her head, underneath her chin. Her legs were bent at the knees and her lower legs were crossing back and forth. "Should we leave?"

Gillis was smiling at the younger cadets, "No, we can go over to my place."

"No, I should probably go home," Doernitz said. He was lying across from Zapata, on his side, started to stand up. "I am sure it is getting really late."

DuBravac held her hand out in a stop everything motion, "No, we will go over to Les' dorm room. We have to, um, feed Cosmos anyway. You two stay here."

"Are you sure?" Zapata asked, her voice betraying that she wanted to spend more time with Doernitz.

DuBravac looked the two over. No wrinkled clothing, no hair out of place, which probably meant no sexual activity in all the time they had been in the room. "We are certain. What have you two been doing all this time?"

"Talking," Zapata said shyly. "Then we started

going over some of the new engineering research papers together and then we decided to play chess. Why? Is something wrong?"

Gillis and DuBravac looked each other in the eye. They were both thinking how Zapata and Doernitz were very similar in their interest in engines and technical manuals. That was one of the reasons that a woman as attractive as Zapata had problems with men, she was cerebral in her approach to things whereas most of the male cadets were physical or sexual. The Doernitz kid seemed to be as intellectual as Zapata and they shared similar interests.

"No, nothing wrong," DuBravac assured her friend. "You two kids keep playing and we will catch up with you at the wedding and then the bonfire celebration."

Zapata and Doernitz watched the couple leave and the door slide shut behind them.

"Were they acting kind of strange?" Doernitz asked as he studied the chess board. Zapata had him, he knew. She had just taken his Queen.

"Yes, I guess they thought you would have left by now."

"Do you need for me to leave?"

"No, please stay," Zapata told him. She had not had

this much fun with a man in her life. She wanted him to stay as long as he could.

Gillis and DuBravac walked rapidly out of the building and toward the men's dormitory building with Preston following. DuBravac recalled her first date with Gillis, which had not been a date at all.

"Les, do you remember when you first met me?" DuBravac asked.

"Of course dear." Gillis put his arm around her. "Why?"

"I was thinking, you met me at a bar, at a Sorority Sister function," DuBravac was reminiscing as she looked up at the stars in the sky. "And within an hour you had me in your room, screwing my brains out."

"You were absolutely irresistible," Gillis smiled, remembering the first time he laid eyes on DuBravac. "When I first saw you, I knew you were the one."

"How? Was it the fact I was wearing a halter top showing off my cleavage or was it my short skirt?" DuBravac hit him on his shoulder. "Before we went to the party that night, I told Julia Steiner that I was going to dress as sleazy as I could so that I could meet the man of my dreams."

"And did you?" Gillis stopped and embraced her.

She kissed him tenderly. "Oh, yes. I sure did."

Gillis also fondly remembered that night and when he saw first saw DuBravac. She was standing in a crowd of other women with Steiner and Lincoln. He bought her a drink and everything happened so quickly. Gillis recalled that he never felt about a woman the way DuBravac made him feel. It was wonderful and Gillis was certain that she was the one.

About four hundred yards north from their position was the cadet graveyard. The lovers were walking, arm in arm as Gillis stopped and turned toward DuBravac. She could see his mind was working by the way his forehead was creased.

"What is it honey?" She asked.

"I should go pay some respects to Dray," Gillis said softly. "I had not been able to bring myself to go back since the funeral. It is just too painful. He was my best friend."

"I can't believe that his family did not want the body."

"True, but Academy had him buried with a headstone in the cemetery over there," Gillis was pointing. "I need just a moment with my old friend."

"I'll come with you," she gripped his hand tightly. She also had wonderful memories of Love-Easter. Her fondest moments were when he was still involved with Yesenia and the four of them would spend their weekends together. DuBravac missed those days as they were full of joy and laughter and so much fun. Gillis and DuBravac walked together hand in hand toward the cadet cemetery. There was a large thirty foot tall gold statue of the Glorious Leader, Vladimir Sikorsky, over the north entrance. Preston followed them at a respectable distance, guessing where Gillis was headed. It was dark now and visibility was difficult without the solar powered lighting. Preston was wondering why the building and street lights had not yet turned on.

While surveying the soccer field, Junior and Ella Ragnarsson picked their spots for the attack. The brother and sister silently made haste back in the direction of the private landing strip where the *Blitzkrieg* was waiting. Ella had on her light intensifier goggles and saw three people walking toward the cadet cemetery. She turned and looked at them.

"Junior, three o'clock, near the cemetery," she said silently. "I see two of the targets. This is too good to be true."

"Which ones?"

"Gillis and Preston. Some girl is with them, it looks

like the DuBravac girl."

Junior stopped in his tracks and observed that no one else was around.

"Three hostages, in case we need them. This is too good to be true. Let's stun them and get them back to the ship."

Ella nodded in agreement. She had read the dossier on Gillis and concluded that of all the cadets, he would be the one that she would not want hunting her for revenge. Eliminating Gillis early would be a good strategic move. In her mind she had wished that there could have been some way to turn Gillis to join the Ragnarsson assassins. She was aware that her wishes on that subject were foolish. Gillis would never betray his friends as he was far too loyal. Ella lamented that fact as Gillis would have made an excellent addition.

The siblings ran at an angle toward the cemetery, approaching from the east. Ella put on her cloak as she moved and was soon completely invisible to the naked eye. Her brother positioned himself to the front of the burial grounds and saw Gillis and DuBravac kneeling at a gravestone. Preston was looking around, about twenty yards behind the other two.

Junior and Preston's eyes met.

Preston immediately recognized the assassin from the digital photographs Lund had given to him earlier. Preston began to draw his laser pistol and was about to yell when he was hit in the back by a laser blast fired by Ella.

Preston spun in circles and collapsed to the ground, his body made a slight noise and Gillis looked up when he heard the thud.

"Frank?" Gillis called out. His heart started to beat faster as he realized there could be danger lurking. He turned his head this way and that, looking all around for Preston.

DuBravac stood up and noticed Preston was nowhere in sight.

"Damn," Gillis whispered to DuBravac, drawing a laser pistol out from his pants pocket. "Get back to the Dorms!"

The two cadets began running but they did not get far. Both of the Ragnarsson's fired their lasers, hitting Gillis and DuBravac. The lovers collapsed and slid for a few feet on the cemetery grass due to their momentum from their forward progress. Ella and Junior ran to their three adversaries and bound their legs and arms with plastic ties.

"Too easy," Ella said as she was scanning the building tops. "If the flood lights had been on we would have been seen!"

"But they were not on," Junior said with a smile on his lips. "Our luck and their misfortune. We need the two men so leave the girl. I will radio for Chretien to come collect her later. Hurry."

Ella nodded, threw Preston over her shoulder and covered him with her cloak. It clearly was too easy. She heard her brother speaking into his holo-com device instructing Chretien to get over immediately to collect the unconscious woman.

As the two assassins were carrying their two targets away they heard something that sent chills up their spines. They both stopped in their tracks when they heard a menacing growling noise from behind them. Both Ragnarsson's turned and saw Papanikolaou, Lewis, Stewart, Ann Harcourt, Fenster, Frazier, Harrison, Farinelli, a few dozen other cadets and a black wolf, baring her fangs and growling.

The cadets had seen the bright colors of the hand lasers from a short distance which prompted Lewis and Stewart to suggest that they immediately investigate. The cadets were all too willing to assist.

"Shit!" Ella hissed when she saw the group of over thirty cadets looking in their direction.

Lewis pulled out a thermite grenade and threw it in the air, intending for it to act as a flare and alert the Marines on the rooftops as well as the other soldiers that Colonel Gorski had ordered stationed inside some of the nearby empty office buildings. She also hoped that the explosion would alert the students in the dormitories. Colonel Gorski and Lund had been correct, Lewis thought to herself. The killers from the dust storm did come back.

Fenster was holding the leash he had attached around the collar of Theodora. He hoped that she would not panic when the grenades exploded. "Steady girl. Steady."

Theodora was sniffing in the direction of Ella and led the way. The cadets and undercover soldiers followed her and Fenster who allowed the Timber Wolf to pull him forward. Lewis and Stewart had their lasers drawn. The thermite grenade thrown by Lewis exploded about thirty feet in the air. The sky brightened with a brilliant flash. Ella screamed as she was temporarily blinded by the blast of fire in the sky due to her light intensifier goggles.

Then the shooting began.

The Marines and soldiers on the roofs of the men's dormitory were immediately jumping to their feet and ready for action. The bright explosion certainly did as Lewis planned, it got their attention.

Ella tossed the burden of Frank Preston off of her shoulder and jumped behind a large gravestone that had the name of William Bragg engraved on it. She had her laser pistols out, one in each hand and was firing at the charging cadets. Her older brother had done the same, throwing Gillis to the ground and rolling behind a gravestone. He saw laser blasts hitting the ground where he had been standing.

Yuri Gorski and Jen Staszko heard the explosion in their dormitory room. They were in the middle of making love and stopped when grenade thrown by Lewis exploded. They gave each other a look of alarm and rapidly threw on their clothes. They rushed out into the hallway and were met by Lund, Michel Evart and his shadow, Zhao. Lund and Zhao had their laser pistols drawn.

"It came from near the graveyard," Zhao reported.

"They are bolder than I thought," Staszko remarked.

"I would have left the solar system if I were them," Evart commented.

"But they did not. They are here again. Let's move!" Gorski barked.

The five ran past many cadets in the hallway that were walking around, asking what was going on. Jack Harcourt saw his friends running for the door and he followed them down the stair case. Several other cadets rushed behind them wanting to see what all the excitement was about.

Behind his gravestone, Junior had his wrist band holo-com device in front of him. He ordered Trevizo and Kulevska to fly the *Blitzkrieg* over and start blasting the Marines and cadets. He then instructed his holo-com to activate the fifty duplicates that were under what was named "Computerized Hibernation."

Junior lamented the fact that it would take about ten minutes for his duplicates to wake up and be fully functional to enter the combat. He and his sister might be captured or dead by then.

The Marines on the rooftop were firing down at the graveyard with laser rifles. The light from the thermite device had been brief and was soon gone. But they had been prepared and turned on spot lights that were installed on the rooftops. They aimed the powerful beams of light down at the graveyard, illuminating the targets.

Ella, with her eyes sight still temporarily damaged, was completely cloaked and was rolling toward the last tombstone she recalled observing. She hit the concrete object with her upper back and crawled behind it. She thought she would be able to hide behind the new large stone with her black cloak around her. She heard some yells as her brother was hitting some of the targets he was firing at.

Junior fired his two laser pistols at the charging cadets. He aimed at the two women with the lasers and hit them both. Lewis and Stewart both crashed to the ground when they sustained laser blasts to the torso. Cadet Farinelli was hit and she slid backwards onto the grass of the graveyard.

Harrison slid behind Lewis like a baseball player stealing second base. He checked her pulse and found to his relief that she had only been stunned. He picked up her dropped laser pistol and rolled to his right, staying low, and was instinctively firing back. He was able to get a short glimpse of the face of Junior and recognized the hired killer immediately. He began firing at the man, determined to make sure that he never returned to bother him or his friends again. Harrison set the laser weapon on the kill switch, concluding that there was no point in taking the man prisoner. If Harrison had his way, Ragnarsson would never escape again.

To his right side, Harrison saw Frazier attempting to dive behind a gravestone as he was hit by a laser blast fired from another direction. The person that fired on Frazier was completely invisible. Harrison rubbed his eyes. Was that even possible? He had never known of technological advancements such as that. He kept his head down and his body as close to the ground as possible and crawled over to Frazier. He checked his pulse and was relieved that Frazier was only unconscious. Harrison pulled Frazier behind a head stone and resumed returning fire.

Junior continued to fire his lasers at the men and women's dormitory rooftops trying to hit the Marines posted there. He hit two, one of them that had the rank of Sergeant on her shoulders, twisted the wrong way as she fell and went over the roof. Her body splattered blood on the paved street below after her body slammed with a sickening sound of her breaking bones. Junior also aimed at some of the flood lights with great success. One by one, the flood lights exploded as he shot them out.

Jurgen Doernitz and Lila Zapata heard the explosion as well. She looked at him with frightened awareness in her face.

"Do you think those bad men would come back?" Zapata asked out loud.

Doernitz jumped to his feet and took Zapata's hands in his and lifted her up. "Yes, and they will be out to hurt our friends. We have to help them."

Zapata was nodding in agreement that they should help, "I don't have any weapons."

"If I can get on board one of the Marine ships that are on the other side of the dormitory, then we will have a major weapon," Doernitz told her. "You can operate the weapons system?"

Zapata nodded and realized that she was running down the hall, with Doernitz holding her hand in his. "Yes, I can do it. I took a class last semester on the weapons systems. You can fly it?" She knew the answer before he responded. Everyone on the campus had been talking about Doernitz and his talents as a pilot.

Zapata remembered that the Marine soldiers had landed near the men's and women's dormitories in several military transport ships. If she and Doernitz could board one and get the vessel airborne, she was certain that the two of them could exact some damage. Her heart rate was increasing with each step. This was not a dream, it was actually happening. As she ran out of the exit to the women's dormitory she could hear the obvious laser battle going on from Cadet Graveyard. Doernitz was leading her toward the several military transport ships in the distance and she ran as fast as her legs would carry her.

Less than a kilometer away, at one of the cadet

landing strips, the thermite explosion was seen by all present. Many cadets had been working on their engines and cleaning their assigned ships so that they would pass the weekly inspection. The sky brightened as the explosion erupted. Marco Andolini and Mary Lincoln had decided to spend some time washing and polishing their one man fighter ships. Other cadets were there, doing the same. Blossom Li looked up at the sky when the fire ball was visible to one and all.

"What was that?" Li called out loudly.

Cadet Dino Black came running toward them from his ship. He was pointing toward the sky, "Did you all hear that?"

Lincoln nodded and swallowed. They had all been warned that the attackers from the other night might return. She looked over to Marco and he had his holo-com in his hand, yelling out to someone that he had contacted after the explosion had occurred. He turned toward Lincoln, Li, Black and several other cadet pilots that were running toward him. He and Lincoln were the two ranking cadets present, so the underclass men and women would look toward them for leadership.

"There is an attack at the Cadet Graveyard!" Marco announced loudly. "I just spoke to my friend Drew

Harrison. He is pinned down behind a grave stone and he said that there are casualties. We need to help them."

"What are you suggesting?" Cadet Lupita Calderon asked nervously as she walked toward Marco and Lincoln. She was in her second year and still tentative in her resolve, as were many of the younger cadets.

"That we all get airborne and give our fellow cadets some cover from above!" Marco answered Calderon.

"Listen up!" Lincoln had climbed on top of her fighter ship and was waiving to the crowd of thirteen cadets that had gathered. "Our fellow classmates are under attack. We have to defend them! Who is with us?" Marco smiled up at her with pride. She had guts.

"I'm in!" Cadet senior Pierre Zerbe yelled out his support as he was already running toward his ship. He had not been one of the best students at the Academy, but his grades were good enough to pass and he was scheduled to graduate with his class in May. He was not about to stand idly by when his fellow cadets were in harm's way.

Sophomore cadets Lupita Calderon, Roy Starr, Tina Martinson, James Cobb, Dino Black, Cara Perez Guerrero, John Gauthier, Derek Regehr and Basil Varek were also running toward their vessels. Marco felt strange in that so many Bragg Gang members would be flying into a conflict by his side.

Tina Martinson had been informed by Admiral Seward that she was grounded due to her mental lapses on the training mission in the Forbidden Region. She had been examined by a psychiatrist that found that it would be in her best interests to pursue another career field as opposed to serving as a pilot. The psychiatrist and Seward had suggested that she consider criminal investigations or military intelligence. She was determined to prove the good Doctor and the retired Admiral wrong. She ran to one of the open small fighter ships and climbed into its' cockpit. She hoped that this event was a way for her to redeem herself and to prove that she belonged. She fired up the engines. Martinson felt in her heart that if she could just do something heroic, Seward would gladly embrace her request to be reinstated into the cadet pilot program.

Blossom Li was already in her cockpit and starting up her ship. She understood that in the journey of life, duty would call upon a person to act. To Li, this was one of those moments. Her parents had taught her that it was the obligation of the individual to act in defense of others, no matter what the odds might be. She knew that her fellow cadets would be defenseless as they most likely would have no weapons to protect themselves with. It was her duty to enter this battle.   Marco had his ship computer open a communication channel between himself and the few cadets that had answered Lincoln's call to enter the battle. "Listen up, choose a wing partner and fly in tight. We need to hit these people fast. They are the same killers that attacked during the sand storm. So do not hesitate to light them up! Let's move out!"

The small one man fighters began to rise in the night sky. Lincoln and Marco pulled their ships next to each other.

Lincoln asked her computer to open communications person to person with Andolini, "Marco, some of these kids, do you think they are up to it?"

"Let's take the lead and show them how to get it done," he replied. "We can draw any fire off the youngsters and build their confidence. They are needed, and so are we. Let's do this."

Chretien ran at full speed to the graveyard and slid to a stop behind a gravestone. He saw from a distance that his new employers were under fire. A squad of Marines had also been attempting to flank Junior and Ella. Chretien, using a rapid fire laser rifle, began shooting at the squad of soldiers. The eleven Marines were blown to pieces by Chretien's blasts. Limbs and other body parts were littering the ground as Chretien methodically killed each of the division members.

The *Blitzkrieg* was airborne and flying at full speed to rescue the Ragnarsson's and Chretien. The Marines and Army soldiers on the roof tops of the two dormitory buildings noticed the large Raumschiff approaching, flying in low. The soldiers recognized that the space craft was not on a course to simply pass over them. It was on a combat run to pass over them and open fire. The soldiers hoped the large ship was on their side. They were about to learn that it was not.

On board the *Blitzkrieg* were the other two Ragnarsson conspirators, Trevizo and Kulevska. They entered the fray and were firing the laser canons from the *Blitzkrieg* at the Marine Corps snipers on the roof tops. Several young men and women were vaporized by the blasts from the ship. Some of the victims' boots or hands were left behind, but the remaining portions of their bodies were obliterated. The soldiers on the rooftops and the ground were no match for the war machine. It was a massacre from the start.

Trevizo and Kulevska landed the *Blitzkrieg* at the southern boundary of the graveyard and opened the bay doors so that their comrades could board the ship and escape. They continued firing laser canons at soldier and cadet alike. Cadet Li Mingjuan had run out into the grave yard area to help the injured cadets. One of the laser canon blasts hit her in the chest. All that remained of her was her shoes, smoking from the energy of the weapon. She never even had the chance to scream.

Junior heard the sound of his Raumschiff approaching. He fired upon the charging cadets, soldiers and Marines and determined that the time to flee was now. He was not accustomed to running, but the cadets and the Marines seemed to be prepared for each offensive.

Junior observed several other cadets running from gravestone to gravestone, attempting to get closer to him. Junior recognized one of the original targets, Elektra Papanikolaou, among the group. He smiled and aimed both of his laser pistols at the gravestone she slid behind. He fired both weapons on kill setting.

The gravestone that Papanikolaou was seeking cover behind exploded when the two laser beams struck it. She was thrown backwards from the force of the blast and her uniform caught fire on the left shoulder. Junior heard the woman scream in pain. Papanikolaou tried crawling behind another one of the large stone markers when Junior fired at her again. His lasers sliced into her right arm in two different locations, just below the elbow and below the shoulder. Her right arm was severed from her body. She screamed and rolled behind another of the headstones. Junior showed no mercy and fired at that piece of stone and caused another explosion. Papanikolaou was thrown backwards about twenty feet in the blast and slammed into another stone.

Junior laughed when he saw that Papanikolaou was no longer moving.

Yuri, Staszko, Michel Evart, Jack Harcourt, Lund and Zhao witnessed the carnage as they were running toward the shooters. The soldiers on the rooftops should have had an advantage, but most of them were now dead. The Ragnarsson assassins were excellent shots, practically never missing a target. Lund and Zhao had their lasers drawn, ready to enter the battle.

Gorski had watched as dozens of soldiers and cadets were either stunned or killed by the Ragnarsson siblings. He was full of anger at himself as he realized that he should have killed Junior Ragnarsson back when he had the opportunity to do so. Gorski ran full speed in the direction of Junior. He watched as the hired assassin was firing at soldiers that Gorski's father had ordered to protect the cadets. Gorski closed the distance between them. Junior fired his two hand lasers at charging soldiers was not facing in Gorski's direction. Twenty feet became ten feet. Then he was a mere five feet away from the cold blooded killer.

Junior noticed that Gorski was charging directly at him from the corner of his eye. Before he could turn and shoot at the charging cadet, Gorski tackled him by diving into the man, wrapping his arms around him and rolled with him onto the surface. Junior dropped his laser pistol from his right hand when he hit the ground and tried to swing his left arm up at Gorski, to shoot the cadet with his other laser pistol. Gorski was faster and hit Junior in the nose with his closed right fist. Junior felt his nose crush and blood flow down his lips and chin. Gorski grabbed Junior's left arm with both of his hands and twisted until the killer dropped the second laser.

Ella watched as her brother's ship, the *Blitzkrieg*, landed just behind the graveyard. Chretien was firing at the charging soldiers, proving to be a better than average marksman. Ella observed many Marines and cadets die as their bodies were obliterated. She began running for the safety of the ship as she heard the laser blasts and the screams of the dying. Ella observed no impediments to her path toward the open bay doors of the *Blitzkrieg*. She was only about thirty paces from the ship when a black animal jumped onto her back and ripped her cloak off her body. It was the wolf, Theodora, which belonged to Dirk Fenster. The timber wolf could do what the humans could not do; she smelled Ella Ragnarsson and tracked her movements. Ella rolled to the ground and turned to face the wolf. She had her two laser pistols drawn. But her reflexes did not prove quick enough. Theodora growled and leaped at the woman and knocked her to the ground.

Ella screamed as the timber wolf sunk her sharp fangs into her right shoulder. The wolf ripped her tunic and tore her flesh. She dropped the laser pistol in her right hand and kicked the wolf with her right knee. Theodora snapped at Ella again and again as the woman continued to kick at her. Ella was able to fire the laser pistol in her left hand at the wolf. The laser blast grazed Theodora on her shoulder. The wolf yelped in pain and rolled off of Ella. Theodora began limping away, favoring her injured limb.

Ella stood and took careful aim at the wolf, "You are dead, bitch!"

As she began to squeeze the trigger with her index finger, she felt the blade of a knife rip through her forearm. The laser blast missed Theodora completely, tearing a hole into the artificial turf of the graveyard. Ella cried out and dropped her laser pistol. She stepped to her right, to avoid another knife slash. Staszko was standing to her left, holding a foot long blade in each of her hands. One blade was dripping with Ella's blood.

"The only bitch about to die is you!" Staszko snarled and plunged at the killer.

Ella dived backwards and drew two knives of her own from her web belt. Ella smiled as she had been looking forward to sinking her knives into someone. She and Staszko began slashing at each other, blades clanging against blades. Staszko dodged several thrusts and jabs by Ella and vice versa. Their blades would constantly meet, and at one point, Ella and Staszko were inches away from one another. Their blades locked together as they stared into each other's eyes.

"I watched them cut the throat open that idiot friend of yours!" Ella sneered, laughing at Staszko's look of anger. "I watched everything from the safety of my security office. Your friend was a fool. He should have just allowed those men to rape and kill the Greek wench. But, no! He had to be a hero! I laughed as they slashed his worthless throat open!"

"I am going to kill you!" Staszko swore as she slashed her knife at Ella in a right arc. She remembered to breath and keep her anger under control. Anger in combat could get oneself killed.

Ella spit in Staszko's face, "You are nothing! You will be buried here, with that moron Love-Easter and the buffoon Gorski. You are all dead!"

Ella kicked Staszko in her midriff with her right leg. Staszko grunted in pain as she fell backwards and rolled.

"I came to the funeral services!" Ella yelled with sarcasm at Staszko. "I was laughing while all of you pathetic insects cried and cried for your lost hero."

Staszko jumped back up on her feet, wiping the spit from her opponent off of her face with her sleeve. "Just keep talking!"

"My only regret was that I did not kill all of you at the funeral!" Ella charged at Staszko. "But that would have been too easy. You were all together, in one place. I could have blown you all to bits with a bomb."

Staszko had been taught by her mother and sisters how to kill with a knife. Her family had been migrants, traveling from city to city in old Eastern Europe. Men would come and go, paying for sex. Families would come and pay to watch knife tricks and acrobatic stunts. Staszko and her family had to fight to survive as they were constantly in danger from robbers, corrupt law enforcement, jealous wives, politicians demanding pay offs and religious zealots. Staszko realized that Ella, in her arrogance, had underestimated her as an opponent. Ella thought herself superior to Staszko. That over confidence could prove to be Ella's undoing provided Staszko could properly use it to her advantage. Staszko stepped into her opponent and thrust her right hand forward with all her might. Ella screamed as the blade ripped into her abdomen. She could feel the cold steel inside her. She dropped her two knives and looked at Jen Staszko in astonishment. She slumped to her knees.

"A gypsy," Ella mumbled, looking at Staszko with disbelief in her eyes. She fell face first onto the ground, her hands holding the large wound in her stomach.

"You are a gypsy's bitch!" Staszko said as she kicked Ella's head with her right foot.

Staszko was breathing heavily and dripping in blood as she looked around her and saw that Fenster had Theodora in his arms and he had tears running down his cheeks. He looked like a helpless little boy. "She's hurt."

The timber wolf was whining in pain.

"Come on," Staszko told him as she shifted her train of thought from one of a combatant to assisting others. "She will make it. Get her to the hospital. It was only a flesh wound."

Theodora allowed Fenster to lift her up and carry her. The relationship between the man and wolf was one of complete trust. Theodora licked Fenster's face as he held her. Staszko was amazed that Fenster really loved that wolf. Thanks to Theodora, Ella was finished. Staszko decided that she loved that wolf, too.

Chretien continued firing into crowds of soldiers, blowing off arms and splitting bodies apart. He never thought to turn and look behind him. Harrison had slowly crawled up behind the traitor and pounced when the time was right. Harrison jumped onto Chretien's back and threw the smaller man to the ground. He began pounding his fists into Chretien's chest and stomach and lifted Chretien up by his neck with his right hand. Harrison ripped the laser rifle out of Chretien's arms with his left. Chretien was struggling for breath as Harrison tightened his grip around his throat. Harrison threw Chretien to the ground, picked him up by his neck and threw him down again and again. Chretien was soon spitting up blood. After the fourth body slam delivered by Harrison, Chretien went limp, his neck broken.

Gorski was oblivious to the other personal battles occurring around him. He continued his fight with Junior as the prolonged struggle continued. Gorski wrapped his arms around the assassin in a bear hug. Junior was able to knee Gorski in the groin. Gorski groaned and Junior hit the cadet on the left side of his head with his fist. In pain, Gorski released his hold on Junior.

Junior knew that the situation was untenable and ran for the bay doors of the *Blitzkrieg*. He was not paying attention to the other battles that Chretien or his sister was involved in. He only thought of himself. He dived onto the metal floor of his beloved ship. He then turned to see that Harrison was pummeling Chretien to death. He also saw his beloved sister fall when Jen Staszko stabbed her. He quickly concluded that nothing could be done for them and pulled out his hand held holo-com device.

"Kulevska! Take off!" Junior yelled. He heard the engines of his ship roaring to life as Kulevska complied with the order.

Michel Evart had been checking on the unconscious Gillis when he saw that the lead assassin was running for the ship. Evart, satisfied that his friend Gillis was only stunned, began to move toward the *Blitzkrieg*. Evart quickened his pace when he heard the engines on the space craft rumbling for lift off.

Gorski stood up and growled. Ragnarsson was not escaping, not this time.

Gorski ran for the ship. If they were to get airborne, Ragnarsson would recruit a new crew of mercenaries and come back again. This had to end now as too many had died. Gorski was filled with a resolve he had never felt before. Junior would not slither away this time.

Junior heard footsteps coming his way, or, rather he sensed the approach of the two opponents. He turned and saw Gorski and Evart diving at the open bay entrance as the ship was already lifting off. Both Evart and Gorski rolled on board as the *Blitzkrieg* became airborne.

Junior pulled out a twelve six inch blade knife from his utility belt, snarling.

"Take the command section!" Gorski bellowed over the rumble of the engine at his friend Evart. "Get this ship on the ground!"

Evart had not wanted to leave Gorski, but he knew that taking the pilot station was the right thing to do. Evart ran from the fight and charged up the stairs toward the upper level of the Raumschiff as Gorski and Ragnarsson began circling each other.

Doernitz and Zapata had taken over a small Army Transport ship that was only about twenty percent of the size of the Super Raumschiff. Doernitz sat in the pilot's seat and Zapata sat next to him in the weapons tactical command seat. Doernitz began running his hands over the computer console before him, turning on the engines and closing the bay doors. Zapata thought that Doernitz looked like a master concert pianist the way he skillfully ran his hands over the controls. Doernitz verbally instructed the on board ship's computer to produce the holographic steering mechanism. He took hold of the green glowing half-moon wheel and began guiding the ship upward.

Zapata turned on the weapons control board and began activating the rocket launchers and laser batteries. "Computer, open targeting displays," she instructed. A green glowing target wheel, similar to a dart board, appeared before her. "Target that Raumschiff in the distance."

"Targeting," the computer responded.

"Prepare to fire on my command," Zapata said with confidence. She looked over at Doernitz as he was directing the position of their ship directly behind the fleeing Raumschiff called *Blitzkrieg*.

Marco and Lincoln were in range of the rising Raumschiff. They both could see the laser batteries of the larger vessel firing rays of death down on the cadets, soldiers and Marines on the planet surface.

"Cadets!" Lincoln announced to the other eleven

small fighters in their group. "Target that Raumschiff. Follow our lead!"

Marco watched helplessly as army soldiers were being blown to pieces by the weapons fired from the enemy Raumschiff. His weapons display began blinking the color blue, which meant he was in range. He fired his lasers in several bursts at the Raumschiff and Lincoln did the same. They both flew their ships in a circular motion around the Raumschiff and watched as Tina Martinson and Roy Starr followed their example by firing laser bursts at the mercenary vessel. Cara Perez Guerrero and Dino Black fired a couple of laser bursts next.

Lincoln watched as the lasers blasts began hitting the Raumschiff. To their dismay, the attack seemed to do little or no damage. The hull showed some scorch marks from each hit but there was no evidence that the lasers were penetrating the thick metal.

"Damn!" Lincoln yelled into her communication device at the other cadets. "That ship's hull must be reinforced somehow. Everyone back off!"

Pierre Zerbe and John Gauthier had already pulled their small ships up and out of range. They fired their lasers before maneuvering their ships to safety, but the streams of energy just bounced of the hull of the *Blitzkrieg*.

On the *Blitzkrieg*, the laser blasts were felt by Gorski, Junior, Evart, Kulevska and Trevizo. Sitting in the weapons command chair, Trevizo swiveled around to another control panel.

"Computer, how many fighter ships in pursuit?" Trevizo demanded.

"Thirteen," came the computer response.

"Target them and fire armor piercing rockets!" Trevizo ordered. He knew that if the rockets hit the small fighters, the pilots would die in the explosions. They would be no match for the power of the launched weapons of the *Blitzkrieg*.

The computer paused for a second and then informed Trevizo that the rockets were firing.

Marco saw the rockets launch from the enemy ship. "Evasive maneuvers! They fired armor piercing rockets! Everyone, rockets headed our way from two o'clock! Back off!"

Marco heard his ship computer warn that a rocket was coming directly at his ship. He swerved in a spiral motion and forced his ship to go into a nose dive at the planet surface. He waited for a few seconds before he pulled out of the dive and flew at a high rate of speed, skimming the surface of the planet. The rocket hit and exploded on the paved concrete of Clovis City, away from any population center, just as Marco had planned. He had been holding his breath and let it out when he realized he was out of danger.

Some of the other cadets were not so fortunate.

Cara Perez Guerrero was unfortunate enough to have two rockets headed in her direction. She cursed and directed her small ship south, in the opposite direction of the rapidly approaching doom. She checked her computer system and determined that both rockets were still closing in on her. She knew she had time to eject and would be able to glide to the surface safely. But her ship would explode and crash on the civilian population below. So Perez Guerrero did something she had never attempted other than in a simulator room. She flew her ship straight up into the night sky. The two rockets predictably followed. She waited until she was several thousand feet above the ground and cut her direction due west toward the Great Protective Wall. She reached down on the left side of her seat and pulled up with all her might on the ejection lever. She was shot from her cockpit and she watched as her ship sped past the Protective Wall and out over the Forbidden Region as she descended to the planet surface. The two rockets slammed into her ship and exploded. She began operating her controls on the right side of her seat and began gliding to the safety of the ground below. She realized that her heart was pounding in her chest so she relaxed and began breathing normally, hoping the others were able to escape the deadly rockets.

Roy Starr tried to fly his ship upwards, away from the approaching rocket. His reflexes proved to be too slow. He screamed as he knew there was no escape. A more experienced pilot might have been able to avoid the projectile or would have ejected to save themselves. Starr did neither and he died as his body was ripped to pieces in the explosion.

Tina Martinson also attempted to avoid the missile that had targeted her ship. She was breathing heavily, just as she had when she crashed her ship in the Forbidden Region. Her forehead and upper lip was covered with beads of sweat. Her last thoughts were that Admiral Seward had been right about her. She lost her nerve under pressure. She panicked and began crying. She took her hands off of her controls and gave up. Had she flown her ship in a spiral move, similar to Andolini's action, she might have survived. Her attempt at redemption ended when the rocket slammed into her space craft. She covered her eyes with her hands and cried out for her father and mother. Her body was sliced apart in the explosion of flesh and metal.

Lupita Calderon had been attacking the Raumschiff when the cylindrical projectiles were fired. One of her laser blasts connected with one of the missiles and it exploded in the sky. The explosion rocked the Raumschiff and actually punctured the hull. Calderon realized another rocket was targeted for her ship and she attempted to evade being hit. The rocket was closing in on her despite her efforts to outrun it. She deduced that her only chance at survival was to abandon her ship. She pulled on her ejection handle on the bottom left side of her seat. She felt the wind in her face as her cockpit protective glass flew off and she was shot up into the sky from her small fighter ship. In a split second afterward, the rocket hit her craft and it exploded.

Calderon felt pain on her left side. She looked over her body and realized she had been hit by several pieces of shrapnel. She was bleeding in her left shoulder, her left arm, and in several places in her left leg and her side. The seats in the small fighter ships were also able to be flown as gliders in the event a pilot found themselves in a situation such as this, when they had to eject. Calderon, using the small controls on the bottom right side of her seat, directed her momentum toward the Cordell Hull Hospital. She needed medical attention since she was losing blood from several wounds. She prayed that she would make it in time. Using her free hand, she pulled out her Holo-com device and contacted her older sister, Reynita. After telling the older Calderon of her predicament, Reynita preached for her to remain calm and that she would track her holo-com. Lupita felt calm, despite her wounds, as she could always turn to her sister for help.

Lincoln had avoided a rocket by flying up into the night sky and turning her ship into a spiral motion. She watched as the rocket slowly faded from view as her speed reached five thousand kilometers a minute. She quickly flew to her left and saw the projectile fly out into the void of space, no danger to her at all. Lincoln quickly flew back in the direction of the opposing Raumschiff. Lincoln had heard some screams and explosions over her communication broadcast, which meant only one thing: that several of the brave cadets that had volunteered to follow her and Marco had been killed. Lincoln grinded her teeth together. She wanted to knock that ship out of the sky and see the blood of the attackers.

Trevizo and Kulevska felt the impact of the explosion on the outer hull. Kulevska struggled with the pilot control panel as the ship rocked left and right.

Michel Evart had been ascending the metal ladder to the pilots section when the explosion caused by Lupita Calderon's lucky one in a million laser shot to the armor piercing rocket caused the hull breach. He lost his grip on the ladder handles and slid down several steps before he was able to obtain a firm grip. He held tight as the ship rocked back and forth.

Gorski was walking in circles, facing off with Junior. Both men had knives in their hands, ready to stab the other. When the hull breach occurred, Gorski staggered backwards and Junior fell into him. The two men rolled onto the metal floor of the space craft. The ship twisted and both men were rolling over and over on top of each other, toward the open bay doors. The surface of planet New Edinburgh was a few miles drop below them. Gorski realized that they were both in danger of falling off the craft to their deaths. As they neared the open door, the ship twisted again and the two men rolled the opposite direction and slamming into the wall.

Gorski kicked Junior in the groin as pay back for the same act earlier. Gorski then swung his right fist and hit his opponent in the nose, harder than he had the previous time. Junior cried out in pain. He responded by slashing his knife at Gorski's chest, cutting through his uniform and leaving a small cut just below the collar bone.

Gorski felt the sting of the knife wound in his upper torso and cursed under his breath.

Gorski continued hitting Junior in the face and was able to break free from him and get back to his feet.

Junior, dazed from being hit in the face so many times, staggered to his feet as well. He reached out with his free hand to hold the wall and balance himself. His face was covered with his own blood. He looked up in time to see that Gorski was charging him. Junior attempted to move, but Gorski had been too fast. Gorski leaped into the air, sailing with his feet in front, and hit Junior in the upper torso. Junior fell backwards and rolled toward the open bay door. He dropped his knife and grabbed desperately for any object to keep him from falling to his death. For the first time in his life, Junior felt terror. He was able to grasp a metal rod on the wall with his left hand and stop his momentum. He had been only three feet away from falling out of his ship and to his doom on the surface below.

Gorski did not waste time. The cadet jumped onto Junior and stabbed his knife into the assassin's left upper arm. Junior screamed as he felt his warm blood running down his arm. He desperately swung his right fist and connected with Gorski's head, sending him rolling off to the left.

Junior crawled to his feet, searching frantically for a weapon. This kid was good, better than anyone he had ever faced. He recalled that his father had warned him that every now and then there would be such a man or woman, well trained, desperate, with a never say die demeanor and full of righteous indignation. Those were the opponents that were the most dangerous. Gorski was proving to be such an adversary.

"Too bad we are not on the same side!" Junior yelled over the sound of the wind and the roaring engines. "We would have made a good team!"

"Screw yourself!" Gorski yelled.

"We could be partners! You could be wealthier than you could ever imagine! Join up with me and my family! You will have more women than you ever imagined!"

"Never!" Gorski growled. "You and your family have killed people I care about!"

"So, you want to serve the Royal Family?" Junior laughed. "I know everything about you! The Space Command killed your mother and you are loyal to them?"

"Don't you ever talk about my mother!" Gorski ran and slid to the ground and took Junior's legs out from under him.

The killer fell backwards and his head crashed on the floor with a loud thud. He felt his skin on the back of his head tear from the impact. He saw stars and felt as if his head had exploded. He shook his head and rolled onto his side.

"The military and the government killed your mother and they would not think twice about doing the same to you!" Junior yelled at Gorski. "You fool! I offer you profits! You want to see the universe? I can give that to you! Anything your heart desires is yours! Women! Money! Adventure!"

Gorski kicked him in the chest with his right foot. Junior fell backwards from the force of the impact.

Junior was dizzy and tried to roll away as Gorski, using his knife, slashed his Achilles' tendon in his left leg. The famous assassin yelled out in pain.

Gorski jumped to his feet, grabbed Junior by his hair and slammed the assassin's face hard onto the metal floor. Junior felt his front teeth crack on impact. Gorski pulled out a binding cable from his pocket and tied it to the right wrist of the man and bound him to the metal pipes on the wall.   "You will be prosecuted!" Gorski promised, kicking Junior's knife out the back of the Raumschiff, watching the strong winds catch it and disappear from sight.

"You really are going to give your life and your loyalty and allegiance to the Royals?" Junior asked, wiping the blood from his chin and cheek with his free arm. "They will kill you like they did to your mother! The Space Command ordered your mother to be blown up!"

Gorski pointed his knife at him, "I told you not to speak of my mother again."

"Look kid! You have only two choices. Join up with my organization or kill me. I could use a man of your talents. You are a great hand to hand fighter and resourceful. If you don't join me, then I will just escape again and come back after you. I will have no choice but to honor and finish my contract to kill you. Join my team and we can make money together."

"Your people rape and kill women!" Gorski began walking away to go help Evart if he needed it. "You murder innocents! I would rather be dead."

"Suit yourself, kid," Junior checked his upper teeth with his tongue. One of his upper front teeth was missing.

Gorski left Junior who was laughing hysterically. "Kid! Come back!"

When Gorski was out of sight, Junior pulled open his finger nail and took out a small drop of acid in a capsule. He broke the receptacle open and poured the acid on the binding cable around his right wrist. The acid ate through the metal binder and Junior was freed in seconds. He began searching for his laser pistol and found it underneath some metal seats on the opposite wall. He held it in his hand and set the weapon for a kill shot. Gorski was good, better than him. That meant Gorski had to die.

Evart had made it to the pilot section and found only Kulevska there, guiding the ships controls. Evart pulled out his laser and stunned the traitor. Kulevska fell forward and his head hit the computer control panel. Evart had wanted to beat the man to a pulp for all of the people that had died, but taking control of the ship was more important.

Revenge would come later.

Evart pushed the limp body of Kulevska out of the pilot seat and took over the controls. He noticed from the flight pattern they were nearing the edge of Clovis City. About three miles ahead was the massive protective Great Wall that kept the indigenous monsters from entering and feeding on the human population.

"We do not need to be going in that direction," Evart mumbled to himself and took hold of the steering column. He began to move the ship to the left, with the intention of going back to the Academy and get assistance in arresting the scum on the ship.

Unknown to Evart was that Doernitz and Zapata were in firing range of the *Blitzkrieg*. The two cadets looked at each other and Doernitz nodded to her. They had witnessed the three fellow cadets blown out of the sky by the Raumschiff weapons and they wanted to stop the killers from escaping justice.

"Do it," Doernitz told her.

Zapata pressed the yellow button on her control panel. Two armor piercing rockets launched from their ship and were on target to take down the Raumschiff *Blitzkrieg*.

Trevizo heard the warning alarms in the weapons section that there had been a rocket launch attack on the ship. Trevizo activated the counter-measures in an attempt to avoid the approaching projectiles. He called the pilot section, and received no answer.

Evart heard the requests for Kulevska to communicate from another conspirator. Evart ignored the man, deciding that it was best to let him guess at what was happening. Evart opened communication channels with all approaching craft.

"May Day! May Day! This is Cadet Michel Darcel

Evart in control of the Raumschiff Blitzkrieg! Do not fire upon this vessel! I am returning her to the Hangar Deck so that the conspirators may be arrested. Repeat, please do not fire upon this vessel!"

Doernitz and Zapata heard the May Day.

"Oh, no!" Zapata said looking at Doernitz helplessly. The weapons section did not have the ability to abort or recall a weapon once fired. "We fired on our own!"

Marco had assembled the remaining fighter ships around his. Lincoln was flying in to join them and had counted that there were nine left. Two confirmed cadet pilots were dead and two had ejected. Lupita Calderon was not responding to communications requests. Cara Perez Guerrero had responded that she had ejected safely and would land on the planet surface soon.

The nine heard the May Day as issued by Michel Evart. Lincoln and the others saw the two rockets closing the distance with the Blitzkrieg.

"Those rockets are going to hit them!" Blossom Li said loudly.

"Can we stop it?" Dino Black asked.

"Fire on the rockets!" Marco ordered.

The nine ships began firing laser batteries at the two rockets. But they missed, as the rockets were traveling too fast. Impact would occur in seconds.

Trevizo had a laser in hand and was running for the pilot section. He knew something was wrong as his friend Kulevska would have communicated with him. He made it to the pilot section and found Kulevska out cold on the floor. He charged in and fired at the intruder in the pilot seat. Evart felt the electrical charge hit him. He fell forward and let go of the half-moon shaped steering command and the *Blitzkrieg* pitched forward out of control. Trevizo was thrown toward the front of the ship and he slammed into the protective observation glass of the pilots' section.

Yuri Gorski also fell forward. He was almost to the pilot section and had no idea that Junior was behind him, slowly aiming his laser pistol for a kill shot. The assassin was breathing slowly as he aimed and intended to kill Gorski and escape. He was in the process of pulling the trigger when the two rockets fired by Zapata hit the left side of the *Blitzkrieg*.

The explosions were deafening. The left side of the Raumschiff was ripped open as fire, metal and smoke spiraled in all directions. The ship was caused to move sharply off course, spinning even further out of control. Junior fired his laser pistol at the moment the rockets impacted the hull of the space craft. He was propelled into the air by the explosion and his laser shot missed Gorski who was also thrown upward due to loss of gravity. Gorski slammed against the wall and turned his head back to see that Junior was attempting to aim at him for another shot. Gorski pulled out his knife from the sheath and threw it end over end at the assassin.

The knife buried into Junior's left shoulder, causing him to cry out loud and drop his laser.

Gorski could feel that the ship was out of control. He desperately wanted to get to the pilot section, check on Evart and determine what was going on. But, he had to deal with the assassin once and for all. Gorski was confused; he had cut the assassins left Achilles tendon which meant that he should not have been able to walk around so easily. Further perplexing Gorski was how he was able to cut loose of his bonds. The hired killer was a master of escape and could have been a proficient magician in another life.

Trevizo spun around in the pilot cockpit and saw that the ship was spinning end over end in the direction of the Great Protective Wall which separated Clovis City and the man-eating creatures beyond. Trevizo screamed in terror. If the crash landing did not kill them all, then the creatures below would feast on them. The idea of being eaten alive, the carnal fear of it, had Trevizo in a panic. He tried desperately to grab hold of the steering column to pull the ship out of the certain doom. He knew he had to strap himself in, but the descent was so rapid and the rotation of the vessel made it impossible to get himself secured in a seat. He cursed at Evart. The cadet was unconscious but had secured the safety belts around himself before he had been stunned. Evart would most likely survive the smashing into the Wall but he would succumb to the reptilian and insect population beyond it.

Gorski and Junior were grappling again. Gorski pounded his fist on the hilt of his knife, forcing the blade deeper into Junior's shoulder. The killer shouted out in agony as the tip of the blade was against his metallic bone. Gorski hit the man in the face, over and over again. He had enough of the mercenary.

CHAPTER THIRTEEN

Marco and Lincoln watched helplessly from their fighter ships as the *Blitzkrieg* spun toward the Great Wall.

"Everyone get ready!"   Lincoln ordered the remaining cadets in the small ships. "If they crash on the other side of the Wall, those creatures will be all over them. We need to cover their escape."

"I will land and go after them!" Li volunteered.

"No, I will!" Doernitz answered. "My ship is larger and we can take in extra passengers. Cover us if the ship goes over the Wall."

Marco, Lincoln, Li and Cobb recognized Doernitz voice.

"You little bastard!" Cobb yelled as partially blamed Doernitz for McWilliams expulsion from the Academy. "You fired at our own people!"

"Stow that kind of talk!" Marco ordered. He knew he would have fired as well, had he been in Doernitz' shoes. "Jurgen! We will cover you! Keep your eyes open for Verburgt and Jumpers; they are known to populate this area."

Lincoln began sending distress signals to the Army Corps of Engineers that managed the Great Wall. They needed to be warned. This crash landing could go badly.

Pierre Zerbe sent out a distress call to the Army marksmen on the wall that were vigilant for any flying Cawlers that might attempt to swoop down upon some unsuspecting civilian.

Zapata looked at Doernitz with fear in her eyes, "We are going into the Forbidden Region?"

"Only if we have to," Doernitz told her. "From the trajectory of the ship, it looks like it might hit the wall on the top. If it slides, it might not fall over."

"Might?"

Doernitz shrugged, "I can't be certain. But the *Raumschiff* might just stay on this side of the Wall." He knew he was stating his own wishful thinking.

The *Blitzkrieg* slammed sideways into the Great Wall. The metal on metal collision caused loud grinding noises and some explosions. The front protective glass of the pilot section shattered on impact and Trevizo was thrown from the ship. Trevizo screamed as he fell, head over heal, rotating several times. Trevizo hit the tree lines in the Forbidden Region and slammed into large tree branches that broke his fall. He continued falling, hitting branches as a descended. He felt his ribs breaking which caused him to be unable to breathe. He could taste the blood in his mouth. After what seemed like seconds, Trevizo impacted the planet surface with a loud thud. He spit up blood and struggled to catch his breath. He looked up and saw the face of a curious Dozal staring down at him. Trevizo tried to scream as the creature growled. Trevizo realized there were several of the flesh eaters around him. They pounced on him, ripping him open with their razor sharp claws. His throat let out a piercing cry as he felt his limbs being eaten. He tried to cover his head with his arms, but the Dozal had his lower arms in their powerful jaws and began tearing them from his torso. He was torn to pieces and devoured.

As the *Blitzkrieg* slid over the top of the Great Protective Wall, the metal on metal impact was causing red and yellow sparks which lit up the night sky line. The ship was spinning in circles as the sliding continued. Some army snipers on the wall were crushed to death as the ship rolled over them. A few tourists also died as they could not avoid the large space craft, only blood stains on the wall remained where their bodies once stood. The engineers inside the Great Wall could hear the screeching grind of metal on metal.

Inside the *Blitzkrieg*, Gorski had wrapped his hands into some straps on the wall and he held on for dear life. Junior had wrapped his fingers into the holes on the metal grated floor. The force of the velocity was causing Junior's fingers to suffer gashes. He was gritting his teeth in pain. But it was not courage that made the assassin hold on, it was the knowledge that he would most assuredly die if he were to be unconscious when the ship slammed into the purple sands of the Forbidden Region. He looked up at Gorski and saw the cadet glaring down at him. Junior could tell by Gorski's facial expression and the intensity in his eyes that their struggle would be a fight to the death.

Gorski could feel the strain on his muscles as the ship continued to slide across the top of the Great Protective Wall. He recalled his training in his freshman year at the Academy from the many simulator exercises. One of those courses involved intense conditions similar to a space craft crash landing. Gorski compared the simulated classroom experience to the real thing and concluded that the conditions of an actual collision were far more violent than the simulated one. The force, speed and velocity, although present in the simulator room, could not really prepare one for the violent collision that Gorski had now encountered.

Marco and Lincoln flew their small ships over the Forbidden Region, positioning themselves over the tree lines, waiting to see the final resting place of the *Blitzkrieg*. Li and the other pilots were following them, ready to assist.

Doernitz flew his small Transport ship to join Marco and Lincoln. Zapata's hands were shaking with fear as she had never been that close to the Forbidden Region. Doernitz noticed her shaking and he reached over to her and held her hand.

"We are going to be fine," he assured her. Zapata swallowed and looked out the observation windows at the vast forest of green, brown, red, yellow and other colors. She knew that underneath the sensational spectrum of color that would please the eye of any artist awaited death for those that dared enter.

The velocity of the sliding *Blitzkrieg* was slowed by the safety poles on the top of the Great Protective Wall. A forty foot tall statue of the Glorious Leader, Vladimir Sikorsky, was knocked over by the force of the craft. The large statue tumbled over the side of the wall and slid down into the forest. The Raumschiff hull was pierced many times over as it slid across the top of the wall. Slowly, the torn vessel came to a stop.

Gorski realized the ship had not fallen over and released his grip on the safety straps and dropped to the metal floor. His arms were aching from the intensity in which his muscles had been tested. Now was not the time to relax, as he had to finish Junior once and for all.

Junior began to stand up, but Gorski was on him, not allowing him the chance to go on the offensive. The cadet kicked the assassin mercilessly in his ribs and again in the stomach. Junior tried to roll away from the onslaught that Gorski was unleashing on him, but the cadet was relentless. He continued kicking the killer multiple times. Junior was coughing up blood as Gorski's kicks had caused some internal damage.

"How? How did you escape again?" Gorski demanded as he grabbed his tunic and lifted him up with both hands. "I cut your Achilles! You should not have been able to walk around like you did! Speak to me!"

Junior spit blood in Gorski's face, laughing. "My legs, they have metallic rods in them so I don't need my tendons. As far as how I escaped your bonds, that is my business."

Gorski dragged the killer to the back of the ship to the open bay doors and saw that the opening was facing the dreaded Forbidden Region.

Gorski threw Junior to the metal floor and pulled out his holo-com and spoke into it. "This is Gorski. Anyone copy?" As he spoke, Gorski pinned Junior to the metal floor with his right knee in his back.

Marco and Lincoln were over joyed to hear his voice. "We are here my friend!" Gorski heard Marco's voice. "Jen, Drew and Lund are almost to the ship. They stole a transport and are landing now."

"Good," Gorski said. "We may have a few prisoners here."

"Yuri," Lincoln said softly. "Starr and Martinson are dead. And they shot Elektra. She was hurt really bad."

"How bad?" Gorski could feel his rage growing. Of all the Gorski Gang members, Elektra was perhaps the most innocent of all. She was also well liked by all of the members due to her pleasant demeanor and caring attitude toward others and for Gorski, she was like a little sister to him.

"She is not expected to make it," Lincoln informed him.

Junior was laughing as he had overheard the conversation. "I shot the bitch with my laser. She had no business stabbing the Rosenburg kid. When she did that the order was given to take her out and she became a legitimate target. I told you, I will kill all of you."

"You son of a bitch!" Gorski snarled as he tossed his holo-com aside and grabbed the assassin by the tunic, lifting him back to his feet. "She was innocent! So were Martinson and Starr!" Although Gorski had never really been too close to the dead cadet pilots, Starr had been one of the trainees in Gorski's company. Accordingly, he felt responsible for the young man, even though Starr had also been a member of the Bragg faction. Gorski and his friends had several altercations with Bragg and Starr, but the kid did not deserve to be killed. The major source of Gorski's rage was that they had shot Elektra.

"No one is innocent!" Junior defiantly shot back. "We all deserve death! That little tart was a witness and had to die. I saw her during the battle and shot her. And you know what? When she dies, I will be at her funeral. I will watch all of you cry and weep over her grave. And I will laugh at all of you. That is my greatest joy in life, watching the loved ones of my victims crying like babies because I killed a person they loved. It is the most wonderful feeling, knowing that I make such a difference in the grand scheme of things."

"She never hurt anyone!" Gorski yelled in his face.

The two men heard footsteps as Lund, Zhao, Harrison and Staszko carefully walked onto the back of the space craft.   "Is he the bastard that shot Elektra?" Harrison asked, aiming a hand laser at Junior. His face was showing a mixture of anger and stress. Harrison had watched as Jack Harcourt had rushed Papanikolaou to a medical transport after he had found her lying twisted on the ground. Harcourt had been fast in acting on seeking help for the girl and used his powers as a Child of Athena to keep her heart beating. Harrison and the others continued the pursuit of *Blitzkrieg* as the wounded were airlifted to the hospital.

"I confess!" Junior laughed at them. "All of the death and destruction was my doing! Lock me up! I will only escape again! I will come back and kill another and another until all of you are dead! There is nothing you can do about it!"

Staszko had a long knife in her hand and was ready to use it, "Let me cut his heart out!"

Lund was silent, aiming his laser pistol at the assassin.   Lund had decided he would allow Gorski to handle the situation. It was time for Gorski to show what he was made of.

"You deluded fools!" Junior was clapping his hands together as he taunted them, "You really believe that any of you matter? Each of you are nothing! Your friend Elektra was nothing! She is lucky, because I finished her off quickly. Each of you will die badly, that I swear to you."

Gorski growled and lifted Junior up over his head, one hand holding the man's tunic at his chest, his other hand on his belt. Gorski's arms were throbbing from all of the strain from the crash landing, so it was a struggle for him as he carried the laughing killer to the edge of the bay doors and looked down at the Forbidden Region.

Junior realized that he may have pushed Gorski to the point of no return. The cadet was actually going to throw him to the flesh eating reptiles and mammals below.

"Wait a minute!" He yelled, trying to claw at Gorski with his hands. "Let's talk about this!"

"You're killing days are finished!" Gorski yelled and threw Junior out of the back of the ship. He watched as the man responsible for so many deaths dropped rapidly toward the trees of the Forbidden Region. Harrison was proud of his friend for showing no mercy to the man that had shot so many soldiers and fellow students.

Junior screamed as he fell toward the forest below. He was astonished that Gorski had it in him. He hit the trees and felt the limbs crash into his body as he fell down to the purple colored sand below.

Lincoln, Li, Marco, Black and the other cadet pilots observed from their small fighter ships as Gorski threw the screaming man to the Forbidden Region below. They watched Junior's arms were flailing and his legs were kicking the air as he rapidly descended to the planet surface.

Lincoln closed her eyes. She had once loved Yuri Gorski and knew in her heart she loved him still. He had been a man that, despite his faults, had always believed in the rule of law. Now Gorski had just committed an act that was contrary to everything he had believed in. She wondered what it was that made Gorski break and ignore his own values. Or had it been a combination of events? Lincoln knew Gorski was the type of man that never verbally revealed his thoughts on things unless he had to. She would never be able to pry out of Gorski why he snapped and killed the assassin as he was generally a very private man. Lincoln shuddered, knowing that she most likely would have done the same to the man that had shot Elektra.

Junior landed hard onto the surface. It took a few minutes for him to catch his breath. He felt his ribs and winced in pain. As if he suddenly remembered where he was, he stood up quickly and looked around his surroundings. He quickly determined he needed to get back behind the safety of the fifty foot tall Protective Wall, so he began running for the structure. He also opened his middle fingernails and began pulling out two flame darts. He hoped that he would not need the weapons, but he had them ready just in case.

As he ran rapidly toward the metallic engineering marvel, he heard hissing behind him. He looked over his shoulder to see a six foot tall red colored reptilian creature, standing on its' hind legs. It was obviously curious about him. It had a large mouth with sharp teeth. Junior could see the four claws on each of its' upper hands, they were long and sharp. The arms were about two feet in length and much skinnier than the two muscular hind legs. He recognized the beast, it was one of the reptiles called a Jumper, due to its' ability to leap long distances. The scientists on New Edinburgh had given the creature another technical name, which escaped him at the moment. The bottom line was that they were deadly and known to be aggressive. The Rosenburg family had captured a few

Jumpers and used them in their Arena to kill uncooperative slaves or enemies.

He stopped his run, turned and quickly judged the distance between himself and the Jumper. He threw a flame dart at the Jumper creature which connected the upper torso and in seconds the monster was incinerated.

Junior was smiling when he turned back toward the Great Wall. What he saw between him and the Wall wiped the smile from his face. Another dozen of the Jumper creatures that were all similar in size to the one he had just killed, were facing him making hissing noises. He recalled reading somewhere that they traveled or hunted in packs. He immediately threw his last flame dart and roasted another one of the creatures. He had hoped that by killing another one, the rest would be scared off and flee. He started running the opposite direction and felt one of the surviving creatures jump onto his back. His plan had failed as the creatures were not frightened away. If anything, his flame dart attack only angered the other Jumpers.

Junior screamed in terror as the Jumper stabbed its' claws into him.

The creature ripped the flesh off his back. The other creatures were on him. He felt his right arm torn from his body. As he screamed, he was flipped over on his back. His stomach was shredded as the Jumper creatures mauled him. He could feel his intestines being ripped from him. Junior Ragnarsson died screaming. The creatures ate the assassin, leaving only the metallic legs and arm implants as evidence that he had ever existed at all.

Up above, Yuri Gorski heard the screams of the assassin as the creatures ate him. Gorski felt Staszko hug him. He held her close to him.

Lund and Harrison nodded to each other.

"Now he is prepared to be an officer in the Space Command," Lund said softly of Gorski.

Harrison took in a deep breath, "I am going to check the rest of the ship for others. And my friend Michel was on board. We need to find him."

Lund pointed to the ladder, "I will go with you. Let's give Gorski and Staszko some well-earned privacy."

The men ascended the ladder and made their way to the pilots section. They found Kulevska's crushed body on the floor leading to the pilot's section. He had been tossed around like a rag doll in the crash. His blood and internal organs were spread over the walls and floor.

They located the unconscious Evart, sitting in the pilot's seat. Lund checked the cadet and found that Evart was breathing but his pulse rate was not steady. Harrison saw that Evart had some cuts and scratches, but overall, he did not seem to be seriously injured. Lund unbuckled the safety harnesses holding Evart to the pilot's seat and lifted the man up into his arms.

"Let's get him to the hospital, just in case," Lund said to Harrison.

The two men departed together, carrying Evart down the ladders. They were ready to leave the wrecked *Blitzkrieg* behind.

"So we won?" Harrison asked hopefully. "This is all over?"

Lund inspected the advanced weaponry and computers as they carried Evart and shook his head at Harrison. "Son, the worst is yet to come."

"But Yuri killed the lead assassin!" Harrison protested. "It is over."

"Did he, Drew? Did he kill the lead assassin? I doubt it. Remember that Ivar warned that his father would come for him. Now that we killed or captured all of these bad actors, I think that the father will be coming. We need to be ready."

Harrison considered Lund's warnings silently and reflected on all of the past events. He could not imagine things being worse than what they had already been through. Harrison shook his head as they made it to the lower level of the ship. If the father of the Ragnarsson's was as cruel as his children, then Lund was correct. They had to be prepared.

As the cadets began to board transport ships to be taken to the hospitals for treatment, Lund and some technicians began to inspect the wrecked ship. When they entered the lowest level, they found the fifty duplication tubes with the green tinted clones inside. Lund whistled and scratched the back of his head at the sight.

"What in the name of Odin is this?" Lund walked around the canisters, looking at each of the faces of the clones inside them. He turned his attention to one of the technicians at the doorway of the chamber, "Contact the Colonel right away. He needs to see this."

"What is it?"

"Something new. Something we have never seen before."

"Should we be worried about contamination?" The technician seemed scared in the way she asked the question.

"I don't know about contamination," Lund told her. "But we should definitely be worried. This is something that goes way past my rank and pay grade. We need to bring in experts to examine this find."

Pursuant to Lund's order, the technician ran back down the hallway to contact Colonel Gorski. Lund looked around at the alien machinery that was mounted on the walls and he looked back down at the fifty tubes. He had a sinking feeling that if they ever learned the answer to what all of it meant, they may regret the day that they dared to ask the question.

"What is this?" Lund asked out loud as he gazed into the fifty tubes.

What he saw astounded him. Each tube had a body inside of a green skinned man. Lund looked closer at the figures and noticed that each one of them resembled the assassin Junior Ragnarsson except that the nose portion of the face was not fully formed. Lund stepped back and shook his head to himself. The assassin, or someone that he had worked with, had come close to perfecting the art of cloning. It was a sobering thought.

"Thank the Stars these things were not unleashed on us in the battle," Lund said to no one in particular. "If they had been, we would have all died."

END OF BOOK FOUR